CW00553971

The Way You See Me

Katherine Bitner

Copyright © 2023 by Katherine Bitner

All rights reserved.

No part of this publication may be reproduced, distributed, or transmitted in any form or by any means, including photocopying, recording, or other electronic or mechanical methods, without the prior written permission of the publisher, except as permitted by U.S. copyright law. For permission requests, contact [include publisher/author contact info].

The story, all names, characters, and incidents portrayed in this production are fictitious. No identification with actual persons (living or deceased), places, buildings, and products is intended or should be inferred.

First Edition: February 2023

Copy/Line Editor: Kimberly Steinke/Parker Mayne Editorial
Cover Design: Melody Jeffries Design

Contents

In loving memory of my Nana, who had unwavering faith that I would someday become an author.

Prologue

The buzz of the needle is a familiar sound. I've sat in several tattoo parlors over the years. Always on the outside though, watching friends and boyfriends get inked up, voicing my opinion of their less-than-desirable ideas. But not this time; this time I am sitting here alone, my arm outstretched before me. Tatted-up hands with thick fingers grip my forearm, digging the needle in deep as I keep my breath steady. The artist told me his name, but I have already forgotten it. I fight the urge to call him Snake, even though I swear that's not what he said. Or maybe I'm just distracted by the snake tattoo wrapping around his meaty neck.

"Kellen didn't want to come with you?" Snake asks me gruffly, breaking my trance of studying his inked skin. His dark brown eyes momentarily flick up to me, and my throat grows hot.

"Nope," I reply dryly, closing my eyes to let the pain of the needle drift me away from the sting of Kellen's name.

He is just another name in a long list of boyfriends who made promises they couldn't keep. I should be used to it by now.

Snake doesn't reply. He barely nods his head. I don't know why I suddenly feel like I need to clarify why *I'm* here, but I do. I open my mouth, and he grips my arm a bit harder. I guess I was wiggling.

"Kellen and I broke up. He was supposed to get an anchor to go along with the compass." A hiccup-like laugh escapes my mouth, making me pinch my lips tightly together. An awkward silence makes the buzzing noise more intense.

He pulls the needle away from my arm, and I look down to see a mostly done tattoo. A simple compass sits etched on my forearm. The piece of notebook paper I sketched it out on lays beside Snake. This should've been the final step before Kellen and I embarked on our trek across the country—all the way to California, where the Pacific Ocean and a group of his friends would greet us. But things happen. People change their minds. They leave when you least expect it.

Snake wipes my tender forearm with a cloth, his touch surprisingly gentle. Maybe he feels bad that my boyfriend of five months left me two weeks before our big adventure.

"You know, an anchor and a compass don't really go together. Unless you're a sailor or some shit." Snake shakes his head and lets out a tiny chuckle, revealing a shiny, gold tooth.

I don't say anything. I only close my eyes as he floods my skin with black ink.

Ten minutes later, my arm is wrapped in what looks like a hospital bandage. I thank Snake, and he tells me to come back anytime, but I exhale with a laugh. In two weeks, I hope to drive away from this city and never come back. There's nothing left for me here.

A dusty-pink sky gently illuminates the sidewalk as I make my way home. I walk past the Thai restaurant, where the owner knows me by name, and rub my rumbling stomach. The thought of Daisy circling my legs the moment I walk through the door makes my legs move faster, and a smile takes over my face. It seems she's been the only one happy to see me for longer than I care to remember. The dull aching on my arm pauses briefly as my eyes land on my other baby parked in front of my apartment. In all her vintage, orange glory, my Volkswagen camper van awaits, eager to see the world. It's not going to happen the way it was supposed to, but regardless, this van will be my home in two weeks.

As I reach for the dented and dirty front door, ready to shower and crash, my phone buzzes with a number I don't recognize. I hit ignore, but they call back immediately.

"Yes?" I answer, annoyed. I'm about to hiss into the phone that I will pay tomorrow when a familiar, soft voice meets me on the other end of the phone.

"Scarlett, it's me, honey. Now don't worry, but I'm in the hospital . . ."

The rest of his words are drowned out by the pounding of my heart.

Chapter One

I push my pink sunglasses up the bridge of my nose for the hundredth time, disgusted by the amount of sweat dripping from every part of me. The driver's side window won't go down any further than halfway, just like the owner told me it wouldn't when I bought this van a month ago. But that doesn't deter me from desperately winding the manual window crank, vying for more wind on my face.

"Oh, thank God!" I yell out, slapping my sweaty palms on the torn, leather steering wheel, my eyes focusing on a glorious road sign ahead. Asheville is two-hundred miles behind me, and I've been coasting on empty for longer than I care to admit. I should've stopped earlier, but the last thing on my mind was putting diesel into this relic of a vehicle. Judgment seeps from Daisy's eyes as she turns to look at me. Her tongue flops out the side of her mouth, saliva dripping down to the floorboard.

The van sputters and jerks as I roll into the gas station

on fumes, and I slam it into park. Daisy grips the front seat with her paws, but it's useless. All sixty pounds of her falls forward toward the dashboard. I reach out to try and break her descent, but it only results in my freshly inked arm getting pinched between Daisy and the dashboard.

"Ouch! I told you to sit on the floor, Daisy!" I cry out, but I instantly recoil and reach to pet her.

Daisy is unphased, though, her eyes searching the empty station. She hasn't listened since the day I picked her up from the shelter. But I only blame myself for that. Her past is unknown. I was only told that she was found as a starving and fearful stray, so it's been my mission to fill her life with abundant love.

I still remember the day I met her. It's crystal clear in my head. I had just moved to a new apartment after a breakup. While scrolling online, I saw someone post a picture of this scared little thing, and within the hour, I was at the shelter. I spent another hour sitting outside her kennel, telling her all about me—about my new tiny apartment, the shows I like to watch, the parks I'd take her to, and about Gramps. I told her she would have a grandpa who loved her just as much as I would. The staff might've thought it was strange, but they didn't say anything. I wanted to gain her trust. I knew how important that was. She came around eventually, putting her paw through the metal link door and pulling on every heartstring I had. I brought her home that night, and ever since, we've been inseparable.

Leaving Daisy in the car, with every window down, I pump gas and jog into the convenience store. It takes everything in me not to moan with pleasure as the cold air blasts down my neck. A gangly teenage boy at the register looks away from me, uncomfortable, as I pull my sticky shirt away from my chest to let the air dry my dampened bra. I beeline for the drink cooler, stacking ice-cold water bottles into my arms.

"Is that it?" the cashier asks.

"That'll do it." I raise my eyebrows in response, handing him a crinkly damp twenty from my pocket. I cringe as he smooths it out.

"Sorry, I don't have AC."

He glances up at me, then turns to look out the window at my orange van. Handing me my change, he says something robotic, then I trudge back into the blazing, southern sun.

Daisy greets me with a thumping tail. I pour water into her bowl while promising her I will install both heat and air in the van as soon as I have the money. In response, she lets a mix of water and drool drip from her mouth, painting the inside of the passenger door.

"Two hours left, girl. Time for a little Stevie?" I toss the empty water bottles into the back of the crowded Volkswagen, rip open a beef stick with my teeth, and peel out of there, turning Fleetwood Mac on full volume.

I was never one for practical things. Old, forgotten, and seemingly useless stuff calls my name. All of the stuff in my apartment are found treasures. My roommate calls it junk. I know Gramps will be full of opinions about my old van, being the sensible man he is. But I love the van's orange paint and white trim. It reminds me of the creamsicles I used to devour behind the house when I was a kid. I also love that this van had a life before me, giving me hope I will create my own stories in it one day. And even though Daisy refuses to be anything but a shotgun rider, there is plenty of room for her in the back since I've ripped out all the seats.

I had a plan to work on it during the two weeks leading up to my departure date, but I got a call. And the man on the other end of the call takes priority over everything. I've waited seven years for this trip. What's one more unexpected delay?

Stevie Nicks's raspy voice is soothing as I roll along the interstate to the shore. It's hard to believe it's been six months since I've been to the Outer Banks. The day after Christmas, I left, promising myself and Gramps I would figure it out this time. *It* being a steady income, a place to live, and cutting out toxic people. But it's easy to break a promise when you can hide. Gramps doesn't drive far, certainly not hours to Asheville, and I was always *busy*. Busy making drinks behind the bar for disorderly customers, busy scrambling for rent, busy avoiding a roommate who couldn't stand me, and busy falling into crappy relationship after crappy relationship. *Busy* makes it easy to stay away.

I had left the tattoo parlor at seven on Friday night, and by seven fifteen, I was on the phone with Gramps, having him tell me again and again what happened: he'd suffered a heart attack.

He was taking the trash out Friday morning, and it hit him. That's what he said. Gramps told the story like he was telling me how he takes his coffee every morning, like this was some run-of-the-mill situation. He didn't want to call me until he knew I was home from work, which made me feel like an even crappier granddaughter. Maybe he thought I was too busy to come, or maybe he thought I wouldn't be much use if I did. But I would've dropped everything and driven all night to be with him. Regardless, he made me promise to wait until Sunday when he was expected to come home. so I didn't have to see him hooked up in a hospital bed, especially after I'd spent months in a room like that with Mimi. I promised, but after hanging up, I clung to Daisy as she licked the salty tears streaming from my eyes.

I let go of Daisy and looked around my dingy bedroom. I knew I wouldn't sleep that night. But after only an hour, I had finished shoving everything I owned into garbage bags. My roommate barely blinked an eye as I walked into the kitchen with raccoon eyes and opened a cabinet. Two plastic cups from the bar I worked at sat on top of a stack of paper plates. That was the extent of my kitchen belongings, so I slammed the cabinet shut and went back to my room. I wouldn't be coming back once I left. There were only two weeks left on my apartment lease—aka the handshake agreement I had with the greasy man who owned this basement apartment.

By lunchtime the next day, I walked to the bar to quit the job I had only started a month ago. Another thing that's become routine in my life.

By Sunday afternoon, I was rolling down the highway, driving as fast as I could. Once the mountains disappeared in the background, I didn't look back.

I inhale until my chest fully expands. "I missed that smell, Daisy." My eyes flutter shut for a moment, relishing in the indescribable smell of ocean air.

Daisy tilts her head, her limp tongue falling out of her mouth. Technically, Gramps lives on the Sound side of the islands, but Daisy doesn't need to know the details; all she cares about is curling up on Gramps's leather sofa and running on the beach. I drum my fingers on the wheel. The ocean will do me well too.

After nearly eight hours of driving, and as the sun starts to set, we arrive at the little shingle-clad beach house in the Outer Banks. As soon as I kill the engine, I lean forward, gazing up at the living room window. The glow makes my heart race.

"Let's roll, Dais—"

She hops out behind me, stretching her stumpy body before bounding up the steps to Gramps's front door. She remembers him. Or she remembers the copious amounts of beef jerky he slipped her at Christmas.

"Gramps, I'm here!" I knock but push the door open anyway. Daisy shoves past my legs, nearly knocking me over.

My smile fades into an awkward gape as I'm startled by a man with two remotes standing in front of the TV. Readjusting my posture, I unstick my hair from my damp neck and shut the door softly behind me. I wasn't expecting visitors, but I should've known better. Gramps makes friends everywhere he goes, and everyone loves him.

He looks up at me from his green recliner, his face breaking into a wide smile. "Scar, my girl! You're here!"

His smile makes my eyes well up, but I suppress my emotions and shuffle over to him, wrapping my arms around him as he slowly stands. Gramps's hug is strong, and it comforts me instantly to feel his arms around my shoulders. I almost expected the heart attack to diminish him into a frail, old man. Daisy breaks up the reunion, pushing between us to get some attention.

"Yes, yes, I see you there, Daisy!" Gramps hollers, smiling down at her.

"Hi, Gramps." I grin, tilting my head slyly at the mystery man across the living room. He turns around with an uncomfortable expression on his face.

"I'm so sorry. I'll be out of your hair in a moment. I'm just finishing setting up your grandpa's new TV," he says, walking over to hand Gramps a remote.

His green T-shirt looks like it's a size too tight, and I self-consciously glance down at my own grimy clothes. "A new TV, Gramps?" I turn, tuning out the muscle-clad IT guy.

Gramps holds the remote in front of his face, studying the buttons before pointing it at the massive flat screen mounted on the wall. "Yes, ma'am. You remember Lola?"

How could I forget? She is the only sixty-seven-year-old woman I've ever known with perkier boobs than mine.

"How could I forget?" I reply, not meaning to sound so snarky.

"Well, she's been a real saint, as always. She bought me one of these platinum-screen television sets since I'll be useless for a few weeks. We can get movies right on the TV with a click of a button. Rowan says so anyway!"

Gramps swings the remote around, nearly knocking me out. I duck, wondering if he is loopy from medication or if he needs new glasses.

"Who the hell is Rowan?"

"I'm Rowan," the guy in front of the TV replies with a husky, commanding voice.

I nod slightly at him and cross my arms over my stained shirt. I wonder if I'm supposed to know who this guy is.

"And we're all set, Ray." Rowan smiles at me and Gramps. "It's a pleasure to meet you," he says, extending his hand toward me.

I shake it weakly, hoping he'll leave now. No part of me was prepared to see anyone but Gramps, especially not a guy like Rowan. "You too," I mumble before turning my attention back to Gramps as he settles back into his recliner.

Rowan makes his way to the door with Daisy trailing him. She's always desperate for attention. "I'll be back tomorrow to get that doorbell camera installed, but if you need anything at all, I'm just a holler away, Ray."

Gramps waves at him nonchalantly.

"Daisy, come!"

She waddles to me, reluctant to listen. Not many people are excited about hippo-sized pit bulls following them around. "You don't need to come back, Rowan. I'm here now, so I can take care of the doorbell. Just leave the instructions out."

A stifled, gruff noise makes me whip my head around to catch Gramps rolling his eyes. "Scarlett, you tried to set up my cell phone, and I couldn't make calls for a week." He shoots Rowan a wink. "Come on by tomorrow, son. I couldn't go anywhere if I wanted."

Rowan nods seriously, but his eyes are warm. "I'll be back tomorrow, sir. See you around, Scarlett."

"Mm-hmm" is all I muster up as he closes the door behind him. Gramps narrows his eyes at me quizzically, and I slink into the sofa next to him.

"What's up with you?" His eyes are trained on me.

Daisy jumps up on the sofa, curling up on my legs. My fingers instinctually make their way to her velvety ears, and I shrug. "I'm just tired, but I'm happy to finally be here."

And I don't trust any man but you right now. So let's please not discuss the hot handyman you've befriended.

Gramps doesn't say anything else, so I attempt to get into caretaker mode—whatever that may mean.

"Have you eaten dinner yet, Gramps?"

"Yes, I have. Lola brought me salmon and potatoes. She made some for you too." He points at the kitchen.

"How nice," I reply dryly.

Lola loved to make food for me when I visited, which was convenient considering she is Gramps's next-door neighbor. She also loves her acrylic nails and spilling the tea when you don't ask. But Gramps seems to like her company, and she looks out for him, so I promise myself to keep my comments minimal. She was here, and I wasn't, so I can't really say much.

"Here, let me help you." I grab the remote from Gramps's hand and click until I find the History channel. Gramps looks pleased, pulling the lever to recline in his seat. I still don't understand why Rowan thought installing Netflix would be helpful for him. Gramps watches the local news, the History channel, and buys DVDs if he wants to watch a movie. He doesn't need all that.

"It's so good to see you, kiddo." Gramps's blue eyes crinkle as he smiles.

I swallow the lump in my throat. It's so good to see him. My heart hurts thinking about how long it's been. I can't help but feel like I've fucked up.

"I was so worried about you, Gramps," I whisper back, afraid I'll cry if I say more.

"Don't worry about me. Good as new, and I haven't been alone a minute since Friday."

I try to smile but just end up blowing air from my cheeks. He could lose both legs in a shark attack and still would say, "I'm good as new." That's the kind of seventy-five-year-old man he was.

"Okay, but are you sure that guy knows what he is doing? I mean, what cable company sends out a technician on a Sunday night?" Rowan looked too fit and clean-cut to be someone who hooks up TVs and installs security systems. Not that I know. I barely know how to connect my Bluetooth headphones.

"Rowan? Oh my word, I thought I was the one losing my marbles. You don't recognize him?"

When I shake my head slowly, Gramps rubs his jaw, pondering.

"I suppose you only met him once before he deployed." Gramps scratches the thick tuft of messy, peppered hair on his head. "Well, anyway, Rowan is Lola's nephew. He got out of the military a few months ago and is staying with her. You'll be seeing him around."

I narrow my eyes as I mentally rake through my memories. There's only a faint remembrance of him from a few years back.

It hardly matters now. I quit my job and drove all the way here to take care of my Gramps. I may not have my own life together, but when it comes to Gramps, I have to believe I am capable of this.

Chapter Two

The alarm chimes at nine, two hours past when I planned to get up. I've been trying to wake up earlier, but it's been no use. Especially since I don't get home from work until three in the morning and Daisy likes to snuggle up on my legs, making the task of leaving my bed impossible.

Unlike my old apartment, Gramps's house is quiet as I meander into the bathroom. I'm both relieved and slightly grossed out to see nothing had been touched in the guest bath since I'd been here at Christmas. I try to comb my hair, but I have forgotten how the humid, salty air makes it wild. I lean into the mirror and pull my hair up and down, looking at my sandy-blonde roots. Lately, I've been dying my hair a rosy pink, which I think looks nice with my summer tan. Gramps calls it cotton-candy hair, and coming from a sweet tooth like him, I figure it's a compliment.

A hot and steamy shower awakens me, clearing my

brain fog. It dawns on me halfway through my shower *why* I wanted to wake up early in the first place. I quickly turn the faucet off and hop into clean clothes. My wet hair drips down my back, and my clothes stick to me as I scurry out onto the front porch.

"Son of a—" I slam the side of the house with my palm and jump as Gramps clears his throat. Sitting in his rocker, with an unbuttoned, faded, denim shirt, he flashes me a funny grin. Mimi would cluck her tongue at the both of us if she saw how disheveled we look. But she'd do it with a smile, like always.

"Rowan beat you to it, kid. It's neat, huh? It can see people, you know?" Gramps says enthusiastically, pointing at the camera neatly installed next to the front door. He brings his hand to gently rest on his stomach. Gramps has always been fit, but lately he's been putting on some weight.

I hold my groan as I slump into the rocker next to him. "Well . . . isn't that just so helpful of him." I *should* be grateful Gramps is being looked after.

"He's just trying to help, Scarlett. He's a veteran, you know? Served two tours overseas. Lola was worried about him when he came home. Says he doesn't like to be idle. So we've been putting him to work," Gramps replies with a chuckle.

"I see. Well, I'm here now, Gramps. Anything you need, I can do it," I reassure him as he sips his coffee from the Snoopy mug I got him for Christmas a decade ago. "Hey! Wait! You're not supposed to be having caffeine." I stand, arms crossed over my chest.

He waves dismissively, with the twinkle in his eye I missed so much. "This here " — he rattles the stained white mug—"this is decaf, young lady. Lola got it for me.

It's fine. One little cup in the morning is fine."

I sit, only to bounce right back up upon hearing pawing at the door. Daisy bounds out, jumping directly off the deck into the yard. She is either full of energy or sleeping like a rock; there is no in-between for her.

"Daisy is still unhinged, as you can see, but I think she's happy to be here. It's better than my basement apartment. That's for sure." I fidget in the rocker. I wish I could give her more. "Daisy is the strangest dog I've ever known. But she's a loyal thing," I say, and Gramps doesn't take his eyes off me. His mop of peppered hair is combed back, and I have the urge to stand up and hug him again, but then he speaks.

"And how are you, Scar? I've missed you. It's quiet without my girls around."

I swallow. He means me and Daisy, and although it's been five years, I know he *also* means Mimi.

Gramps and Mimi raised me from the age of six. Their only daughter skipped town without a trace, leaving me with her aging parents. You'd never know it, though. Right where my mom left me, my grandparents picked up, with more energy and love than my mother could've ever provided. I grew up with them in Wilmington, but when I left for college seven years ago, they finally retired to the Outer Banks.

Even after Mimi passed, Gramps was a spitfire. He did everything himself. I know hearing his doctor tell him to slow down after the heart attack is a hard pill for him to swallow, but I'm hoping I can distract him by being here. And maybe make up for some lost time before I leave again. Because I always end up leaving again.

I finally answer his question, after hollering for Daisy, who's started digging a hole in the sand. "I'm good,

Gramps. I finally got my van." I gesture toward the Volkswagen sitting in the driveway.

What I don't tell him is how I drained my savings to buy that van a day before Kellen decided it was over. My thought was if I got it, if I saw it every day in the driveway, then maybe I'd finally do it—the trip I've been wanting to do since high school, the one that keeps being delayed for various reasons.

"You know I believe in you, Scar. You're Mimi's granddaughter through and through, which also means you're stubborn as a mule."

"Wait, *I'm* stubborn as a mule? Speak for yourself," I tease lovingly.

He throws his head back, laughing. We exchange quirk smirks.

"Scarlett Ray, you *are* stubborn. That *thing* looks like it needs something done. I don't know what, but something. I want you to bring the van up to Lu's Garage in Kitty Hawk. He'll make sure it's safe," Gramps says, his tone becoming fatherly and serious.

"I don't think I can really afford to fix anything—"

He interrupts my train of thought with a stern glare, and his bushy brows furrow over his bright, blue eyes. "You don't worry about that. I can't let you drive a vintage piece of metal that might break down."

I nod in defeat even though I'm full of gratitude. I'd let him help me, but I made a promise to myself that I'd pay him back. It would be slow, but I'd do it.

Over the last seven years, I've mentioned my plans for a trip out west to Gramps and Mimi. First, I was supposed to embark with my friends from high school, but everyone went off to college, and the trip was deemed *outlandish*. Gramps paid for me to go to college too, but

I didn't make it past the first year. I was too distracted and had too much time with a bottle to my lips. I've since straightened out, but my thirst for the trip never waned. I had boyfriends who promised to make the trek with me, even one who almost went all the way, only for them to get cold feet the morning before we were supposed to leave.

All I ever wanted was to drive through the mountains, see the expansive desert sky, and dip my toes in the Pacific Ocean. Mimi and Gramps never discouraged me from this dream, but seven years is a long time to hold on to something that keeps slipping from your fingers. The van was my last attempt to muster some courage, to prove I wasn't lying to myself.

"All right, so what's on the agenda for the day, Gramps? I'm here and at your service. Do you need groceries or anything from the pharmacy?"

He rocks next to me while sweetly patting the top of Daisy's head. My eyes linger on the aging skin of his hands, which somehow look five years older than they did at Christmas. I have to peel my eyes away from his face. I've always thought of my Gramps as spry and kick-ass. He wasn't frail, but this heart attack definitely scared him. And it scared me too. It was minor, and it was a miracle how quickly he got treated. But still . . . it's too painful to think about him getting older. Especially after Mimi's passing.

He must've sensed the thoughts in my head. He always was annoyingly perceptive. When I was a kid, it meant I didn't get away with anything, but now, as a grown woman, it means he can read me like an open book.

"Lola got all my groceries for me, and the pharmacist brought me my meds yesterday," he says, smiling down at my goofy-looking dog.

I forgot how small this island town is. Everyone knows everyone, and the pharmacist is an old friend of Gramps. Lola is Lola, but it's nice to know Gramps has a fridge full of food.

My leg bounces while I search my brain for something helpful to offer. "I can make you something, then. A panini, or even Mimi's tuna casserole?"

My suggestion brings a grin to his face, and he turns to me. "Since when do you know how to make Mimi's casserole? I don't recall you ever listening to Mimi's instructions when she cooked."

I gasp comically, causing Daisy to perk up and spastically leap onto my lap.

"Daisy! Dang, girl. I can't breathe!" I push her off me but instantly pull her back to me, kissing her face. She's somehow managed to be both my whole heart and the bane of my existence. "I have made it a few times in Asheville. Don't you worry about me now. It's decided. I'm making it for dinner."

"All right, Scarly Ray. You do that." He finishes the last bit of coffee in his mug, then pushes himself carefully out of the rocker. "I'm going to rest for a little bit now."

I jump to open the door for him and slowly walk behind him as he moseys to his recliner. I know better than to ask him if he needs help. He'd tell me I am being ridiculous. I pretend to be busy looking in the refrigerator, but I peer over the door as he adjusts himself in the recliner. He lets out a yawn. He'll be out like a light in minutes.

I chuckle. Some things never change.

Chapter Three

E ven as a kid, I was all over the place. It's as if I've been training for a transient life since I came out of the womb. The school even told Mimi I had attention issues, but she refused to take me to the doctor. Mimi said the good Lord gave me extra energy for a reason, and she wouldn't have some doctor tell me I needed pills to correct that. I don't know if she was right or wrong, but I do know she made me believe it was my superpower and that my lack of concentration was something unique about me. In many ways, she was right because I didn't fit in all that well at school. I was the wild child who talked too fast and too much for most kids my age.

Mimi also made her own herbal tinctures and swore by a medicinal book of remedies passed down by her grandmother. She made me drink teas and tinctures to help me concentrate, and I hated it. But now I'd do anything to see her in the kitchen, working over her book and jars of herbs.

When I was younger, I thought my own mother had become addicted to Mimi's tinctures since Gramps was always saying Mom loved her "herb" more than anything. Now I know what kind of "herb" he was talking about.

We didn't talk about my mom often after she left. Mimi became my mother, and Gramps was the best father I could've ever imagined. It was a random day in July when my mom left and never turned back, but I don't remember much about that day to be honest. It was a routine day: my mom dropped me off at summer camp, and Mimi picked me up. But this day, Mom never stopped driving after she left me. I wondered where she went, but the reality was that my grandparents were more involved in my life than my mom ever was, even before she skipped town.

Even though that day forever changed our lives, Gramps still has a framed photo of the four of us on the fridge. It's a time capsule in a magnetic plastic frame. It's been there for decades now, but my eyes always glaze over it. I don't need to look at it. That photograph can't give me closure.

After breakfast, I sift through the cabinets, taking inventory of the ingredients I need for dinner. It's only noon, and Gramps is still napping, but I have nothing better to do. Plus, I'm getting restless. A trip to the grocery store sounds fun right about now.

I change into my favorite jean shorts—or what I call my comfort shorts because I wear them more than is acceptable. They are so worn-in that the denim is bare in certain areas, but I've remedied it by sewing patches on. I have an eagle, a rose, a smiley face, a dog face, and a "Future is Female" one. Gramps has deemed them my crazy shorts.

"You stay here, Daisy. I'll be right back," I whisper to my dog as she emits low, rumbling snores in sync with Gramps. Outside, the air is sticky with humidity, and I crank the windows the minute I get in the van. Some days I'd consider selling my left arm to have AC in here.

To kill time, I turn left and drive to the grocery store that's further away, the one tourists go to on the main stretch of land. The windows are down, music cranked, and I'm driving up the main, two-lane drag, barely topping twenty-five miles per hour in the traffic.

Dogs' heads pop out of car windows, prompting me to make a mental note to take Daisy to the beach tomorrow. Maybe Gramps will want to come too. He loves to fish, and he used to love to swim in the ocean, but age has slowed him down a bit. We could take chairs and let the water rush up to us while Daisy runs.

Traffic comes to a standstill at one of the only traffic lights in town. I slide my sunglasses down my nose and squint at the man jogging toward me on the side of the road. Dark blue shorts, no top, glistening with sweat—I stare for an unacceptable amount of time at his impressively built chest as he comes closer, until someone honks and my eyes jolt back to the road. *Fuck!* Slamming on the gas, my tires loudly screech forward, drawing the attention of the sweaty jogger, who makes eye contact with me as he runs by. My stomach bounces off my rib cage, and I snap my face to the road.

Rowan. Freaking Rowan.

He *would* run in sweltering heat down the busiest road

in the Outer Banks at the busiest time with no shirt, flexing his muscles.

I keep driving on, slowly, but my eyes betray me to steal one more tiny glance out the rearview mirror.

Even from behind he looks good.

A puffy breath leaves my chest. I slurp my iced coffee. I used to run too. Well, I tried to do it for about a month. I bought new shoes, a fancy watch, everything. But then the weather got cooler, and it was easier to curl up inside than jog in the chilly morning, so I gave up that hobby. One boyfriend told me I have shiny-object syndrome because I'm always bouncing from one exciting thing to the next. I didn't think that was bad, but he did. He stuck around just as long as my running hobby.

"You're going to spoil me. It smells just like Mimi's casserole." Gramps waltzes into the kitchen, beaming at me like it's Christmas morning. He's changed out of his denim shirt and into a festive shirt that looks like it's more appropriate for a cruise ship.

Daisy presses her tan body harder into my leg, her nose twitching in the direction of the oven as if she didn't just get a handful of treats from Gramps an hour ago. I nudge her gently out of the way to crack the oven and check on the casserole. I hate tuna. The idea of tuna and noodles cooked in mushroom soup makes me gag, and I'm not sure if Gramps ever liked it either, but Mimi made this every Sunday after church, and I know it's comforting to him.

"It's almost done! I'll set the table." I grab two plates

23

and two glasses as Gramps walks to the fridge, pulling out a pitcher of tea I made earlier. "Don't kill me, Gramps, but that's not sweet tea." He shoots me a glare, like I told him I killed a man.

"Before you object, it's *sweet*, but just with a little honey and not how you're used to it. Maybe the mountains of sugar you used to pour in there have something to do with your heart attack." I raise my eyebrows.

He crosses his arms. "All right, fine. What about dessert, though?"

I point to the bowl of chopped-up fruit on the counter and the whipped cream next to it, mustering up my no-nonsense look. Gramps shakes his head, but from the corner of my eye, I see him smile.

"You're going to need to grab two more plates and cups. We have guests tonight," he mumbles to himself. The oven timer goes off at the same time three rapid knocks sound at the front door.

My head whips in Gramps's direction. "You didn't!" I hiss out at him, my eyes glancing toward the front door, and I clock his rare, wrinkle-free shirt.

Gramps gives me a coy look and shrugs like a little boy in trouble.

"Yoo-hoo! Ray! Scarlett! We're here!" Lola's raspy voice fills the silent house.

Gramps breaks eye contact, perking up to greet our *guests* in the foyer.

I watch as Daisy contemplates staying near the food or greeting the guests too. I silently mouth "stay" to her, but even my own dog betrays me, prancing into the other room.

Four plates, four glasses, and a pitcher of tea balance in my arms as I attempt to push the sliding door open with my foot. The kitchen table is too small for four of us, so I decide we will dine on the screened-in porch.

"Here, let me help you." Rowan appears out of nowhere, his hand outstretched for the pitcher in my hands.

I swivel just out of reach and flash a quick smile, but I don't look at him. "I got this, thanks," I reply, awkwardly pushing past him to the table.

He stands behind his chair while I set the table.

I glance up. "You can sit."

"I can wait."

"Well, there is no need. Sit," I reply, setting the empty plate down in front of him. Mimi always insisted our guests sit first. But I have no experience with hosting, and I'm sure it shows.

Rowan's gaze traces me up and down until our eyes meet, holding for a beat too long. Long enough that I register the flecks of gold in his caramel-brown irises. Nonchalantly, he pushes his dark hair off his face, and I stifle a chuckle. Tall, dark, and handsome—that's how he'd be described in a romance novel. Not that I care about labels like that. I'm more of a psychological-thriller gal anyway.

"Scar—oh, how wonderful to see you home!" Lola breaks the tension, trailing onto the porch, followed by a smiling Gramps. Daisy is quick on their heels.

Lola proceeds to throw her arms around me, and I'm overcome by perfume. It's as if this woman said yes to every person who wanted to spray her at the department store. Gramps winks at me over her shoulder, and I raise my eyebrows. He knows I find Lola . . . *pestilent.*

Dinner is served, and Daisy continues to betray me as she lays diligently under Rowan's feet. He says he doesn't mind and he thinks she's a sweet dog. I guess that's something we have in common.

"So Scar," Lola addresses me.

I smile at her, stabbing my fork into another nauseating bite of tuna noodle casserole.

"How is Asheville? I haven't been to the mountains in years. It's so beautiful out there. You must love living there."

I don't look up from my plate. "It's fine. I've been there for nearly seven years now. Kinda ready for something new at this point."

Her face lights up, and she puckers her lips, making an "oooh" sound. "So what I'm hearing is maybe you'll stay here at the beach? That's new scenery!" She laughs at her own line, and my eyebrows shoot up.

"Um . . ." I breathe deeply, and tension builds in my curled fingers, but Gramps comes to my rescue.

"Actually, Scarlett has a trip coming up. Out west! That's why a hunk of metal is sitting in my driveway." He smiles and winks at me.

My heart flutters and falls. I haven't brought it up since I got here yesterday because I've pushed the trip out of my mind. Gramps is the priority, and the last thing I want him to think is that I don't want to be here.

Rowan has stopped eating and is giving me his full, undivided attention. I swallow the tuna, but it's dry going down my throat.

"Where do you plan to go?" he finally speaks.

"California. That's the end goal," I say softly, still not looking at him.

"You're driving all the way to California in that van out front?"

My eyes snap to his, and I'm met with a serious face. I clench my fork a little harder.

"Yes, I am," I reply curtly, taking a long sip of iced tea. Rowan purses his lips

"Why? You have something against 1979 Volkswagens?" I smile tightly.

"Well, no. They are classics. But I heard it sputtering today on the Byway. You're not worried about it breaking down when driving thousands of miles?"

I should've known he'd realize it was me today. Who else has pink hair and drives a vintage orange van? That also meant he probably saw me knowingly violate him with my eyes. *Oops.*

"It'll be fine," I reassure him, shifting my weight in my chair. These aren't even details I've discussed yet with Gramps.

"So when do you plan on going?" Lola chimes in.

Heat tingles the back of my neck. "The plan was to leave from Asheville next Friday. So I guess . . . eleven days from today? But we will see how things go," I add awkwardly, glancing at Gramps. The heat continues its climb up my neck and face.

"Lu's going to look at it soon. Make sure it's safe," Gramps cuts in.

Why would Rowan care if I break down halfway there? Last time I checked, we are not friends. He's nothing more than my Gramps's neighbor's nephew who runs without a shirt and sets up elderly folks' TVs.

Lola smiles and sets her fork down. All the plates are empty.

"Surely, though, your parents must be worried about you taking a solo trip?" Rowan pipes up.

Our eyes meet, and I bite the inside of my cheek. His question brings an unfamiliar tightness to my throat.

"No, my parents don't care about anything." My voice

cuts through the air, causing a silent tension to settle over everyone.

The wooden chair scrapes against the ground as I push back and start grabbing plates. Lola starts to get up to help me, but I snatch everything before she can. "I got this. You're our guest. I'll be back in a minute with dessert."

I keep my eyes straight ahead as I push through to the kitchen, dropping everything into the sink with a thud. The light chatter outside is drowned by the pounding in my heart. Rowan isn't aware my mom ran away or that I never knew my Dad. How could he be? But it doesn't make the question sting less. Didn't anyone ever teach him it's impolite to stick his nose in other people's business?

Dessert was silent. Well, on my end at least. Lola babbled on and on about how Rowan was helping to renovate her bathroom. Apparently, along with knowing how to install things, he can also tile floors and paint. Lola is smitten with her nephew. That much is clear. And Gramps is smitten with Lola, her fake boobs, and her insanely white smile.

Rowan thanks me for dinner three times before he leaves. Once the door shuts behind them, I walk to the guest room and change into stretchy shorts, ready to relax and watch a movie with Gramps.

When I look out the living room window, Rowan is snooping around my van. He's peering into the back, which is full of crap from my apartment. Then he squats down to inspect the front tires. He's either a common thief or a mechanic. Before I go outside to say something, he stands up and walks back into Lola's house. I shrug it off.

Halfway through the historical drama Gramps swears we never saw—but I know we did—he says, "He doesn't know about your parents, Scarlett. Lola didn't tell him."

I grab another handful of popcorn and nod nonchalantly at him. "Okay." I flash a quick smile at Gramps, and he turns his attention back to the movie.

Chapter Four

S torms keep us cooped up most of the afternoon. I forgot how much I love listening to the thunder roll in over the waves, breaking the heat for just a little while. I also forgot how much Daisy *doesn't* love it. Her eyes search the room, distrusting this place and the noises outside as the thunder rolls in and crackling lightning illuminates the sky.

"It's the fifteenth, right?" Gramps looks up from his crossword puzzle at the kitchen table, his glasses low on his nose.

"Mm-hmm. Wednesday, the fifteenth." It's been three days since I got here. Not even a week since Gramps's heart attack. Though it's killing him to sit around, I know he is more tired than he lets on.

"What's a four-letter board game name . . . starts with *C* . . .?" He brings the newspaper closer to his face.

"Clue," I say, sipping coffee.

"Genius. You're a genius, Scar!" he exclaims, penciling

in the answer. I smile to myself, ignoring the fact that an eight-year-old could've solved that.

"You want me to drive you to your doctor appointment tomorrow?" I ask him, looking at the calendar on the side of the refrigerator.

"That's already tomorrow? All right. I guess I should go." His voice fades as he gets back into his crossword puzzle.

I stand silently a moment longer, watching him focus on the puzzle. When I was younger, he'd do them every Sunday morning after church while Mimi made lunch. I'd sit at the kitchen table with him, and occasionally he'd let me help him with one. Mimi would hum a hymn we heard in church, and Gramps would tap his foot along, seemingly absorbed in the paper. But I'd catch him stealing glances over the newspaper, adoringly peeking at Mimi in her yellow, ruffled apron.

The clouds break, and the sun peeks out around four o'clock, an hour before Gramps likes to eat dinner. My restlessness is also peeking out, and Daisy whines at my feet with her leash in her mouth. I scratch her head, grimacing at my fingernail polish that's been chipped for weeks.

"Ray! I'm here, doll!" the familiar raspy voice rings out from the front door, and my eyes shoot back to Daisy's. I swear she rolls her eyes in unison with mine.

Gramps runs his fingers through his messy hair as he shuffles past the living room to greet Lola. A moment later, I'm pushing myself off the sofa that has consumed me for the last six hours and wave at Lola. She is carrying a platter covered in plastic wrap.

"I made you lasagna, Ray!" she yells at Gramps, even though he is only a few feet behind her as they move to the kitchen. Her perfume wafts into the living room. She clearly doesn't know the meaning of subtle.

Gramps fawns over her mother's lasagna recipe as Lola goes on about some gossip she heard at the grocery store this morning. It's obvious Gramps could care less about the drama as I hear his "Hmm" and "You don't say?" from the living room. He's mastered the art of fake listening.

"This is our cue to leave, girl," I whisper to Daisy, and she responds with a tiny wiggle, tapping her paws on the wood floor. I slip on my sandals, throw my hair into a quick braid, and grab my car keys.

"All right, Gramps, I'm taking Daisy to the beach to run!"

Giggles come from the kitchen.

"We will save you some lasagna, hon!" Lola yells. A cabinet slams shut. For a tiny, Italian woman, she has some force behind those arms.

"Be safe, Scar!" Gramps calls out after her.

With Daisy on my heels, we get in the van and drive down to the far end of the beach, where it's less crowded.

"Now, Daisy, you have to listen to me, okay? No running off like last time. I brought your ball and your favorite duck treats. But only good pups get a treat. Understand?" I speak slowly, cranking the sticky gear into park.

Daisy looks at me, then rams her body into the door. She leaps out of the car as I grab her leash. A Jeep pulls up to park behind us, and I glance at the couple in the car. All smiles, holding hands, and giggling.

Give it six months, then it will be all downhill. I

sigh as the cynical thought pops into my head. Mimi always warned me that bitterness is like a parasite: hard to remove once it takes hold. It's hard not to be bitter when the list of people you trust dwindles down day after day.

I clip the leash onto Daisy's collar, and she immediately yanks me toward the walkway connecting to the public beach access. Sometimes I look at her and think, *Wow, she is my only friend.* She hears me voice all my bitter thoughts, and she was there for me through all of my crappy breakups, the rom-com movie marathons, and the endless baths and face masks to make myself feel okay again.

But then sometimes I thank God she *is* my only friend. People judge, but Daisy doesn't. She doesn't care if I love watching romance dramas but suck at real-life relationships. She doesn't care if I get takeout five nights a week or if I spend all of my savings on an impractical vehicle. Daisy also doesn't care that I'm twenty-five years old and have never held a job for more than a few months. She just loves me for me—in all my messiness.

I let out a sigh when an empty beach comes into view. There aren't a lot of houses this far down, and the few that still stand were left boarded up and unrepaired after the last hurricane. I lean down and cautiously unclip her leash, giving her sweet face a stern look before setting her free. She reacts with a few pounces, then darts for the ocean, making me crack up. As Daisy runs free, a warmness spreads in my chest.

Shells and driftwood cover the damp sand, but I kick off my sandals anyway and place them on a piece of washed-up wood. My feet carry me to the water, where Daisy bites at the white-capped waves rolling in.

33

The storms have made the air thick and hot, and a stickiness coats my skin. I remove my shirt and bask in the breeze rolling over me. My black sports bra makes me feel athletic, even though the most exercise I get is my daily walk with Daisy. Thinking about all the hikes we would be able to take on our trip out west together makes me smile, though.

If I still go . . .

My gaze shifts to my neon-pink toes in the water as a wave crashes over Daisy. Her eyes go wide before she starts a mad dash down the shore.

"Daisy! Come here!" I call out in an equal panic.

My maternal instincts are zilch, except when it comes to this four-pawed creature. Her body pauses momentarily as she turns toward me, but a noise catches her attention. I know the look on her face well. It's the same one she gets when she sees a squirrel. I could throw an entire honey-baked ham at her and she wouldn't break concentration. She's already bolting down the beach by the time I lunge forward to grab her collar.

"*Mother fucker!*" I grit out and begin to chase her, trying to dodge the sharp shells with my bare feet.

A man is running toward us, and Daisy is running straight toward him. My lungs burn as Daisy continues to sprint, her legs barely touching the ground like she is some sort of award-winning racehorse. Gramps always jokes she is a greyhound stuck inside a pit bull's body. The joke's not so funny right now.

"She won't bite!" I yell out between breaths. "Just grab her collar!"

Daisy bowls right into the poor jogger. It's a guy. *Wait.* Dark hair. Navy shorts. No shirt.

I let out an audible groan, though it jumbles with the

other sounds I'm making, making it actually sound like I'm dying.

I slow down as I continue walking toward Rowan and Daisy with my hands on my head, trying to steady my heartbeat. My chest heaves, and I wouldn't be surprised if my boobs popped right out of my sports bra.

"This yours?" Rowan jokes, squatting down, petting Daisy like she is a *good girl.*

Her tongue is out, panting, looking at me smugly. *Little devil.* I glare back at her.

"Yep . . . that's mine. Thank you," I get out between breaths. I glance at Rowan, who's watching me. He barely shimmers with sweat or appears like he's struggling to breathe. *Must be nice.*

"She's pretty damn fast."

"Yeah, she is. Not sure how. She spends half her life on the couch under a heated blanket with her Lamby."

"Her what?" Rowan replies, with a small smirk.

He has really nice cheekbones. *Shut it, Scar.*

I don't even hesitate in answering. "Her Lam-eee," I pronounce slowly. "It's this stuffed-animal lamb I bought her after I adopted her from the shelter. She won't destroy it. She just carries it around with her. It's disgusting but adorable."

Rowan says nothing but glances at Daisy, then me.

"Don't judge me," I snap, but he grins widely. "Because I could judge you for running so much. But I don't."

Rowan laughs. "I'm not judging you. I think that's great. She's got a Lamby. And thanks . . . for not judging me for exercising." He raises his eyebrows.

"I just mean you run a lot. I've been here for three days, and this is the second time I saw you run."

"I run every day. It's good for you." Rowan winks. I

think. Or he blinked really hard at me.

"Right, okay. Well . . ." The maybe-wink jumbles my brain, and I can't think of anything normal to say, so I lean forward to grab Daisy's collar, but when I get close to Rowan, I notice his leg. He senses my pause as my eyes linger on his scar.

"Nasty thing, huh?" He runs a hand through his hair, ruffling the top of it.

"Oh, umm . . . No. Does it hurt?" I try to keep my voice cool. Daisy wiggles from my grip and runs toward a piece of driftwood the size of a small tree. Her body instantly starts using all its might to try to pull it down the beach. It's not budging, so I turn my attention back to Rowan.

"No, not anymore," he replies calmly.

"Can I ask how?"

"Iraq, two years ago. Just the wrong place, wrong time." Rowan runs a finger up his calf and thigh. The gesture of his finger dragging on bare skin causes a tingle on my own. For a moment, I allow myself to wonder what his hand would feel like trailing up my leg.

"I'm so sorry. But hey, you're out here running, so that's great." I give a thumbs-up and instantly cringe internally. This is why I stick to talking to my dog all day instead of people.

Luckily, Daisy is acting like a fool. I point over my shoulder at her, and Rowan nods, smiling at both of us.

"I, uh, have to go." I turn back to Daisy, who is *really* trying to drag that damn piece of wood toward the car. Her paws dig into the sand, and my bare feet are ready to turn and take off after her—again. She's already a hundred feet from me, so I yell out to her, "Drop it, Daisy! We can't take that back!"

Rowan lets out a gruff noise, and I turn to him, opening

my mouth to clarify I'm not a bad dog mom. I don't know why I feel like I need to justify when I typically don't care what anyone thinks. I mean, I hardly even know him.

"I'd take it home for her, but the back of the van is full of my stuff," I explain, my hands on my hips, swiveling.

"I'm not one to judge."

If Rowan and I were in a bar right now, I'd assume he was flirting with me. But there's no way someone as nice and well-groomed as him would even be interested in someone like me. Someone with messy pink hair, who chases her dog down the beach and doesn't have a home.

"Well, I *really* have to go. Your aunt made *lasagna*."

"Why'd you say it like that?" he retorts, stretching his arms across his chest like he is getting ready to do an intense workout.

"Like what?"

"Like you hate lasagna." Rowan bites his lip when he replies, causing a hiccup in my heartbeat.

"I didn't. I just said she made it. And I'm hungry. Is that a crime?"

Rowan laughs and shakes his head. "You don't like those two together, do you?" he asks.

"You don't know what you're talking about." I never met someone who asked so many questions, especially ones they have no right asking.

"Look, I've been around here for a few months now. I know Lola is . . . *a lot*, but her and Ray look out for each other. Lola doesn't complain about being lonely anymore, and she hasn't made lasagna for years . . . until recently."

"Well, that's good. I mean, being lonely sucks." I quickly add, "I'd imagine," after catching a glimpse of Rowan's eyes.

"Yeah, it does." He looks at me knowingly.

Tearing my eyes away, I wave goodbye. "All right. See you later, Rowan." I abruptly cut off the conversation with a flat voice and trek back toward my van.

I pause to glance over my shoulder as I drag Daisy away from the driftwood. Rowan's standing still at the edge of the water, his hands in his pockets, looking out over the choppy water. For a split second, I wonder what is going through his head and what he knows about loneliness. But Daisy snaps me back to the moment, jumping on me with sandy paws.

Time to go eat lasagna.

Chapter Five

"Gramps, you ready to go?" I yell out from the kitchen, pouring coffee into a to-go mug. The doctor's office is about twenty minutes away, and though Gramps can drive fine, he happily takes up the offer for my company. We both agree to take his truck, which has AC.

"I'm coming! When did you get so punctual?" he teases, slipping on his leather loafers.

I shrug and open the front door for him. "I figured it was time to start trying to be on time," I admit, realizing I actually have been trying to break my habit of perpetual lateness. It's a hard one to break.

We step out onto the front porch, but I halt dead in my tracks when my eyes fall on the tree-sized piece of driftwood sitting on the front lawn. Gramps looks at me, waiting. I blink rapidly and take a deep breath to regain a steady heartbeat.

"Where in the world did this *tree* come from?" Gramps

kicks it as we shuffle on by to his red truck.

"I have an idea," I reply, my eyes lingering on the sand-coated wood.

"Strawberry with extra rainbow sprinkles for my grand-daughter and a kid's-sized praline for me. Got to listen to the doc," Gramps says wistfully, winking at the girl in the window.

Standing beside him while he orders, I smile, and he winks back, lumbering his long arm around my shoulder to pull me into a hug. It felt like just yesterday I was holding his hand, getting ice cream on the boardwalk. It was always our thing, and our flavor choices never changed.

"How are you feeling about what your doctor said?" I quiz him, taking my cone and immediately biting a dripping pink chunk.

"I feel good. I don't like to take all those pills, but he said I could be back fishing in a few weeks. And Lola's been spoiling me with healthy meals. Did you know there's such a thing as vegetable lasagna? No red meat. Imagine that. Lola's going to make it for me next," he went on, sitting on the bench next to me.

I put my hand on his arm and give it a little squeeze. "Well, I'm glad you have someone to look out for you, Gramps. I wish I would've been here. I would've left the minute you called, you know?" I say, waiting for a reaction.

"It's okay. You're here now. Don't beat yourself up, kid."

I internalize his words.

"Plus, I figured you needed time to let your boss know and whatnot." He takes another bite of ice cream, and I say nothing. The all-too-familiar fear of disappointing him settles over me.

"I was going to quit in two weeks anyways, Gramps, for the trip. And my apartment lease is ending."

"Well, everything happens for a reason, right?" Gramps replies.

I barely nod. I never bought into that sentiment, and I'm not sure he did either.

"So bartending isn't for you, huh?" he pipes up, breaking the silence.

Nope. And neither was waitressing, being a barista, working at the bookstore, or grooming dogs. None of it was for me.

I shrug dismissively. "The boss was sleazy anyway. I'll figure something out."

"You know, you and Daisy can stay as long as you want. The house is too big for me alone."

His wishful tone makes my heart ache. It's just him and me now. Even if I went to California, I'd have to return to North Carolina no matter what. For Gramps.

Squeezing my leg, he turns to face me. "I'm proud of you, Scarlett Ray."

A sharp breath inflates my lungs, flushing my cheeks. That wasn't something I heard, almost ever. Sure, Gramps has told me he was proud—when I got accepted into the college I eventually dropped out from and when I got my first office job that I quit three months later.

"You're proud? I didn't do anything!" I laugh, hoping he's not just saying it to be nice.

"You did. You bought that van. That's a big step toward

41

your dream. And you're here, taking care of your ol' Gramps. You have become quite a woman. Mimi would be so proud."

Tears prick at my eyes, and I wipe them away, casting my gaze over the sidewalk full of families seeking the next tourist trap.

"She wouldn't like the pink in your hair or the new tattoo you think I didn't see." He winks, and I blush, looking down at the compass on the inside of my arm. I'm surprised he didn't mention it until now.

"I miss her," I say, my voice barely above a raspy whisper.

Gramps nods next to me, looking up at the sky. "I miss her too, Scar."

We say nothing as we exchange quick smiles. I scoot over to lean my head on his broad shoulders. We both focus our gazes on the ocean. I breathe in his peppermint smell and allow my eyes to tear up behind my sunglasses. Gramps's face remains tough like it always does. I've only seen him cry twice. Once, a few weeks after Mom left, when the reality of her never returning sunk in, and the day Mimi passed. He was a proud, hardworking man. Sometimes I look at him and, other than the goofiness I inherited, I still wonder how we share the same blood.

Gramps finishes off the last bite of his ice cream cone and claps his hands together, pushing himself off the bench. "All right, back home! Miss Daisy is probably missing you."

We roll onto the sandy driveway and hop out, my eyes

immediately land back on the tree-sized driftwood in the yard. An orchestra of music pulls both Gramps's and my attention toward Lola's house to a propped-open front door.

Lola emerges from her house with a spring in her step, wearing a floor-length dress with colorful birds on it. With her hair in an elaborate twist, she enthusiastically beckons us over. I don't move, wondering if I can escape into Gramps's house before she can catch me, but Gramps beelines for her porch.

"Sounds like you have a concert going on!" Gramps exclaims, taking off his ball cap and pausing on the steps next to Lola.

"Rowan is installing my new shower today!" She smiles and waves at me again, this time more aggressively.

I swallow my groan, thankful for the sunglasses concealing my tear-smudged mascara.

"Scarlett, you look like a girl who likes a beauty regimen," Lola continues, waving her hands around. "So you'd appreciate my new bathroom vanity. You should go in and see what my nephew is doing. The tilework is beautiful. And he put in one of those rain showers. You know, the ones they have in the resorts in the nice parts of Mexico."

"Wow, that's great." My response came out much drier and flatter than intended, even though it was about as excited as I felt about Lola's rain shower.

"Go in and see it!"

She nearly pushes me inside her house, and I awkwardly stumble into the foyer, feeling less and less like an adult who makes her own choices.

"Follow the music!" Lola yells out behind me.

It takes everything in me not to reply, "No shit." I cautiously step over power tools and construction materials scattered across the floor on the way to the bathroom. The music gets louder as I pass through the bedroom door and find the source.

Like an invisible force field that miraculously appears, I halt the moment the walk-in shower comes into view. A quick inhale helps me regain my dignity—and sanity. Inside the enormous walk-in shower, with a caulk gun in one hand and a rag in the other, Rowan stands tall. His tool belt rests low on his hips, and I have to forcefully stop my eyes from following that deep *V* all the way down. Yet again, he is topless. *I mean, does this man even own a shirt?* I'd buy him a damn shirt at this point.

I take another calculated step toward him, stopping in the doorway of the bathroom. My foot *gracefully* lands on a screwdriver, making the loudest clinking sound. Rowan jerks, swinging his head toward me. His eyes look green today, which I only notice because he stares at me with an intense look before cracking the tiniest grin.

I immediately avert my eyes to every other part of the bathroom as I swallow hard. I think about commenting on how nice it looks, but it dawns on me that I've never even seen this bathroom, so I have no way of knowing if this is an improvement—and I'm a shitty liar.

"Lola wanted me to see you . . . I mean this . . . the showerhead. It rains on you or some shit." I stammer over my words and fumble forward, pretending to be very enamored with the box the showerhead came in.

Rowan chuckles and wipes away a bead of sweat from his brow. He leans over to turn the music down a notch. "It's already installed. It's some crazy rain showerhead she spent way too much on, but I'm not here to ask questions." He throws his hands up in defeat.

I tip my upper body into the shower to look at it. It takes all my focus to *only* look at the fixture and not be glaringly obvious about how much Rowan's presence is affecting me.

Being in a shower with any half-naked man would affect anyone, right? Right.

"Nice. What are you here for, then, if not to ask questions?" I ask, pivoting out of the shower quickly. What I want to ask is why was a thirty-year-old veteran living *here* for the summer? But then again, I'm sure he could ask me the same thing.

"I'm just here to help." He wipes the caulk gun with the rag.

"Uh-huh. Okay. Well, good luck with all of this." I look around like an owl and awkwardly turn to exit. Then I pause, remembering the mysterious appearance of driftwood this morning.

"Hey, thanks for bringing Daisy that driftwood. She's gonna go wild when she sees it."

Rowan nods at me, and his full lips gently curve. "Anytime," he says softly.

I quicken my pace as I leave. The moment I get to the front porch, the music in the bathroom goes back to deafening volumes, and I take a deep breath. I hadn't realized I'd been holding my breath.

"Looks great, huh? Rowan is just so handy! He can fix anything." Lola gushes over him as I raise my eyebrows, nodding like a circus clown. *He is so amazing, Lola.* I'm sure that is what she wants to hear.

"It's really something!" I reply, throwing some awkward finger guns at her before leaning in toward Gramps.

"I have to let Daisy out."

He pats me on the shoulder. "Scarlett, tomorrow night

we are all going to The Dancing Swordfish, the new bar and grill on the beach." Gramps smiles and puts his cap back on.

I stare blankly at him for a minute, waiting for some other explanation to come. Not that I'm opposed to beachfront dining . . . but who is *all*?

"Oh, is it a special occasion?" I pop my hip, resting my hand on it. It was beginning to grow unbearably hot in the sunlight. Or maybe it was just my lack of *chill* right now.

"It's my birthday! Sixty-eight years young!" Lola exclaims, pumping her fists in the air.

"Oh! Yay . . ." I muster a smile. I already know what is next.

"You, me, your Gramps, and Rowan. Wear something you can dance in, *chica*. They have live music!" She squeezes Gramp's shoulder, and he turns red. Gramps loves to dance, but I haven't seen him dance with anyone besides Mimi. And me, of course.

I give Lola a thumbs-up, which she cackles at, before she and Gramps turn back to chatting about God knows what.

Galloping back to the house, I leap up the porch steps and rush into the kitchen. With a glass full of water, I push open the bedroom door and sigh a breath of relief. I never realized how much I like being alone.

Daisy yawns obnoxiously and stretches her paws out in front of her, lolloping her head to the side lazily.

"Something I can dance in . . . Great," I whisper aloud to Daisy, repeating Lola's instructions. I grab the remote control, turn on the ceiling fan, and proceed to pull up the menu of The Dancing Swordfish on my phone.

"Well, it's decided, Daisy. I'll be ordering a personal

pitcher of margaritas tomorrow."

Daisy sneezes in response and gives me a judgy look.

"Oh, by the way, your tree is in the front yard."

Thanks again, Rowan.

Chapter Six

The cicadas' buzzing song grows louder as the sun sets. I retire to the front porch to join Gramps, with Daisy following close behind me. I would've come out earlier, but I heard Rowan arrive, and he just left, after what seemed like an hour of lingering.

"Here you go." I hand Gramps his unsweet tea, and he takes it graciously even though I know he doesn't really like it. "What was Rowan here for?" I ask, forcefully keeping my tone casual.

Gramps rocks in his chair, removing his hat and taking a swig of tea. "He borrowed some of my tools for the bathroom."

"Hmm, is that it?" I pry, pulling my legs up under me. I'd only been on the island for a few days now, and already my skin was turning a deeper gold. Gramps and I both tan fast.

I glance at Gramps when he doesn't answer and see an amused look painted on his face.

"What?" I ruse, bashfully looking away.

"He was here fawning over that bull you call a dog. He seems to like her." Though he's speaking about Daisy, he's looking at me like he wants to say something. I turn my attention back to Daisy, who is gnawing on the driftwood on the lawn.

"Well, who wouldn't love Daisy? She *is* the best dog in the world," I reply, still feeling Gramps's eyes on me. Finally, he looks away, and I breathe a little deeper. I know there is something on the tip of his tongue.

"I think he likes more than just Daisy."

There it is! I swallow and purse my lips, rocking my chair a bit harder, before replying. The last thing I'm going to talk to my grandpa about is my love life.

"Oh, Gramps. Of course, he likes you too. You're an old charmer." I look at him with a wink, and he laughs.

"Mimi was better at these conversations—" he starts.

I know where this is going. So far, I've successfully hidden my disastrous dating history from my grandpa. In high school, when I first moved to Asheville, I told Mimi everything. She knew about the guys I dated, the ones who broke my heart, and the ones who I equally destroyed. She knew my track record and my inability to pick the right ones. Mimi never judged me; she listened with an open mind, always telling me to never give up on love. Gramps and I didn't have those conversations. What we had was silent acknowledgment of my suffering. A movie marathon with all the junk food our hearts desired, no questions asked, and unconditional love.

"So I'm not going to even pretend I know the inner workings of a young lady. But you haven't brought home a boyfriend or posted on Facebook about one in quite a while." Gramps looks at me with concern laced in his furrowed brow.

I resist the urge to laugh because I know he is very serious. I only made a Facebook account because of his persistence, but I never actually post anything. Especially not updates on my love life.

"Gramps, I appreciate your concern, but I am *fine*. Really," I reply, pulling at the fringe on my shorts. "I have Daisy and friends in Asheville." It was partially true. I did have friends, but they were not the kind I grew close to. They were the kind who would forget about me the moment I was gone, like I'm sure they already did.

"I trust you, Scar. I just worry about you being lonely. You're out there on your own," he replies, his fatherly voice taking over.

"I could say the same thing about you, Gramps. You're here alone, and I worry about you," I say, changing the subject.

"You don't need to worry about me. My heart is good as gold now." He pounds on his chest comically, and his eyes wander over to the neighbor's home before focusing on me again. "And I have plenty of companionship. I have you and Daisy right now, and my friends keep me good company."

"You mean Lola?" I raise my eyebrows suggestively, as if I'm gossiping with an old lady.

Gramps readjusts in his rocker, crossing one leg over the other and picking up his almost-empty iced tea glass. "Yes, Lola is a great friend," he states matter-of-factly.

"Gramps, you know it's okay if Lola is *special* to you." My heart skips a beat with my reply. It's not something I've yet admitted to myself, the source of my discomfort with Lola. Because when Mimi died, she took half of Gramps and my heart with her. She was a light in our lives, the glue of the family. I never considered how lonely Gramps would be after losing his wife of nearly fifty years. I didn't want him to feel alone, even if it meant Lola entering our tight circle.

"She's a *special* person, Scarlett. But no one could ever be Mimi. Your Mimi Norma was . . ." He pauses, his words catching in his throat. It makes my whole body ache with hurt.

At the same time, Daisy leaps up the front steps, nuzzling her big blockhead under Gramps's hand. Daisy always knows when someone needs her insistent love.

"Anyway . . . Lola is a widower too. Almost ten years for her. We look out for each other, keep each other young. She never had children of her own, just a few nephews. Rowan being here means a lot to her. She'd do anything for that kid. They're good people."

I blink away tears that I don't allow to fall and smile a close-lipped grin at him. It's a hard pill to swallow at times, but seeing him here, happy, I accept it. It would be cruel to deny him that kind of love after everything he's endured. All the loss.

"I know you're not going to stay here long," he starts.

I open my mouth to deny it but stop myself, because I'm not sure he is wrong. This is Gramps's home. It isn't mine.

He continues, holding up a hand to silence me. "Don't deny yourself love either, Scar. This life can be wonderful, and it can be cruel. If you choose to only see the cruel, you'll end up bitter. I say, choose love."

"Gramps, did you read that on the sign in Lola's house?" I look at him very seriously for a moment before we both break into a cackle.

"I did! And I liked it! It's a good saying."

"You're crazy, Gramps."

Daisy jumps up in response to our outbursts and then quickly becomes sleepy, curling up in a ball between Gramps and me as we continue to rock.

I walk inside to get us another fill of iced tea, but as I close the fridge, an old photo in a plastic sleeve seems to glare back at me. We are all standing outside the church in Wilmington, the church we attended for years. Gramps is on the steps with one arm around Mimi, who is beaming in a summery yellow dress. His other hand is on my mom's shoulder, who's standing in front of them. Her long, blonde hair extends to her hips. Her hair is willowy like her figure. And there I stand, my legs splayed like a superhero, hands on hips, hair as long and blonde as my mom's. My sunflower dress was wrinkled, and both knees were bruised from rolling around in the yard with all the dogs Mimi was always rescuing.

I studied my mom's face like I'd done a million times. It was the last photo ever taken with us four and the last photo of her I've ever seen. It was the summer before second grade; I was seven, and she just turned twenty-five, the same age I am now.

"Scarly Ray, bring me a few of those pretzels on the counter, will ya?" Gramps calls out, making me twitch and break my stare from the photo.

Quickly snatching the bag of pretzels off the counter and the iced tea, I walk them over to Gramps with no words and sit back down, desperately trying to hold my thoughts in, desperately trying to shake *her* from my mind. But I can't. She looks too much like me.

I rock back and forth. The sounds of the cicadas and Daisy's snores surround me. The silence between us slowly makes me succumb to my word vomit.

"Why do you still keep that photo on the fridge?" The air stands still the moment the words escape my lips.

Gramps stops chewing before answering, thinking about his answer. "Because that was a good day. You were happy, and Mimi was too. I don't remember from what, but you can see it in the photo."

"Mom wasn't smiling."

"She rarely was. But you were. And that's what matters," he responds with a chipper tone.

A few more beats of silence pass.

"Do you ever miss her?" I ask, my voice barely above a whisper.

He stops rocking and sets the pretzel bag on the table between us, rubbing the salt off his hands. He doesn't answer me right away. I wonder if it hurts to think about it. As I'm about to apologize and change the subject, he opens his mouth.

"I miss the daughter I once had. But she's long gone, Scarlett. You know that. She made her choice, and we made ours. We lost her, but we gained you. I could never wish for anything different because of that."

This time I couldn't resist. I pull my knees up under my chin, wiping the tears that gently stream down my cheeks. "Me too, Gramps. I'd never wish for anything else." I smile at him.

He stands to kiss the top of my head. "I think I'm going to turn in for the night. We have a big day tomorrow. Gotta get my rest," he says.

I laugh through the tightness in my chest, patting Daisy on the rump, getting her to follow me in.

That night, I dream. Mom is there, holding my hand outside the church until she lets it go and mouths something to me that I can't hear. I run after her, screaming her name, but she doesn't turn around or stop. When I stop running and turn around, Rowan's suddenly there, and I crash into his chest. His arms pull me into a hug that feels strong and safe, and I cry freely, letting my tears roll down his chest as he holds me.

I'm pulled from my sleep by a cold sweat, the moon peeking through the blinds, and Daisy hot against my feet.

Chapter Seven

It's the first weekend in a long time I haven't spent at the bar. Between having to socialize and coming home covered in sticky mixes, I'm more than happy not to be there. And after last night's talk with Gramps, I'm happy he is getting out there and being social. His doc emphasized he stays active, both physically and mentally.

I pull out a white sundress and slip it on, waving my hips back and forth in the mirror. I'm not one for ultra-girly things, but the way this fabric clings where it should and flows around my legs, allowing me to move freely, makes me smile.

I'd walked by this dress a million times in the window of an upscale boutique on my way home from the bar in Asheville. Something finally pulled me into the store one day, instead of wistfully looking at it from the sidewalk. The salesgirl told me the dress looked like it was crafted for me, so I ignored the low balance in my bank account and swiped my card.

Looking at myself now, I'm glad I did. I decide to pair it with two feathery, gold earrings, which frame my face. If I'm being forced to dinner, I'm going to at least look good.

The house has been relatively quiet all afternoon. Daisy and I ran on the beach this morning—and by run, I mean I threw the ball for her while my ass was plopped in the hot sand. Gramps was too tired to join us, so he napped and woke up in the nick of time to get ready for dinner.

"Gramps, are you almost ready?" I holler as I gather my phone and my wallet while Daisy circles my legs, probably hoping she's going wherever we are going.

"Yes, ma'am!" He struts out of his bedroom, looking as charming as ever.

Gramps loops his arm through mine and announces that we look dashing. I gush and agree. I'm just happy to see him so spirited.

We stop at a floral shop on the way to the restaurant, and Gramps awkwardly asks me to come in with him to pick out a bouquet for Lola. My heart swells a bit when he pulls a dozen pink and white roses out, smelling them and inspecting each individual one. It was both romantic and so innocently sweet at the same time.

"She'll love them," I acknowledge, and he nods, still admiring them.

We pay and drive on, making our way to The Dancing Swordfish, which was already hopping with tourists and locals alike. It was the newest restaurant in the Outer Banks, with live music and direct access to the beach. I worried Gramps wouldn't be able to handle the loudness and stimulation given how easily he grew tired these days, but the moment we pull up, his eyes light up. He looks like a young man on his way to a dance.

"You look snazzy, Gramps. I like the shirt." I nod at him, and he looks down, acting calm even though I saw him remove the tag from it this morning. He must've bought it just for tonight. I love that even at seventy-five, there are still new things to be experienced.

"You look sharp yourself. Hoping to snag a dance with a certain fellow?" He winks and grabs the bouquet from the center console.

"Not a chance," I reply dryly.

"We will see about that." Mischief is written all over his face.

I don't know what's gotten into him these days. He's always been fiesty, but if he keeps insinuating about Rowan and me, I'll have to start leaving the old geezer at home.

Lola got a table in the corner of the dining deck, overlooking the ocean. Her bright pink dress matches her lipstick and flamingo earrings. It screams "Palm Springs cabana" rather than *this* place, but Gramp's smile reaches the moon when he sees her. He rushes over to give her a hug.

"Happy birthday, Lola," I chime in, unable to deny the sweetness of the moment before I move to take my seat.

Swiftly standing, Rowan pulls chairs out for Lola and me. Like a doting mother, she gushes at him, but I just mumble, "That's not necessary," low enough so that only Rowan can hear. He doesn't look phased though, so maybe he didn't hear.

I prop up the expansive menu in front of my face while Lola and Gramps drone on about this restaurant, the food, and Lola's birthday gifts sent from her friends. The menu covers my face, but I can still see the top of Rowan's head. I keep thinking about Gramps's comments the last few days—how Rowan came to the house for more than Daisy, that he would want to dance with me. It's ridiculous that I'm overthinking my seventy-five-year-old grandpa's opinion on this. Though, he is the one with a better track record than me.

I notice how Rowan's dark hair is perfectly pushed back. Every piece in place. He is somehow both beautiful and rugged. I hate guys who can do that so effortlessly. My hair is pulled up to beat the humidity, but I can already feel a bead of sweat gathering at the nape of my neck, while "Mr. Six-Pack" looks cool as a cucumber.

The waitress comes by, and I slowly lower my menu to see Rowan staring right at me from the other side. His face breaks into a charming smirk as he gazes up at the young waitress, who can barely make eye contact with him. She asks for our drink order, and Rowan starts by ordering a beer.

"And for you, ma'am?" Her brown ponytail bobs as she speaks to me. I notice her eyes continuously glancing at Rowan.

"The margarita pitcher. Lime."

She nods and looks around at the table. "I'll bring a few glasses for—"

"Oh, that's just for me," I interject, feeling the heat of the gazes from everyone at the table. I awkwardly smooth my dinner napkin over my lap, waiting for her to move on. She nods too enthusiastically, and I try to not outwardly cringe.

The thick layer of tension between us is all I can focus on. Lola orders a fruit cocktail, and Gramps asks for water, even though I know he wants whiskey. When the waitress walks away, I look up and catch Rowan giving me a weird look. Maybe Gramps is right, but if he is, this isn't where I want to address Rowan's budding feelings.

My eyes travel up his arms to his short-sleeved button-up, which happens to also be the same color as my linen dress. No one better think we coordinated this.

The waitress comes back in a snap with our drink orders, setting the pitcher for four in front of me. I fill my glass to the rim, and no one says anything as I begin drinking it right away.

"And for you?"

I blink out of my daze, and the ponytailed waitress looks at me expectantly. There is a hint of judgment in her eyes as I sip the margarita rapidly through the straw, and I can't blame her. I have hot mess written on my face.

My mind is not on food, so I grab the menu and point at the first appetizer I see. "The fried calamari looks great," I say, then hand the menu back to her with a friendly smile.

When she walks away, Rowan sets his beer down and leans back in his seat, nodding his head at me. "Not a big eater?" he jokes.

If he did like me, I definitely just ruined that. Who orders a pitcher of margaritas for themselves? A raging alcoholic, that's who. But I can't help that I need something to take the edge off. His presence makes me irrationally awkward.

"Oh, I am. I'm just super thirsty." I cringe at my choice of words, clutching the margarita glass to my chest as I bend my head down to slurp it until it's nearly empty.

"She's a thirst trap," Lola pipes up, and I choke, slamming my margarita glass down and tapping on my chest as Rowan throws his head back in laughter. Gramps looks around at all of us, bewildered.

"Lola, I'm not sure you know what that means," Rowan says between laughs. His hands come up to cover his mouth. I notice his dimples too. *Of course, that freaking perfect face has dimples.*

"Well, all the young people on the internet say it." Lola waves her phone at us.

She isn't wrong. But I'm far from a thirst trap—unless realizing your white, linen dress has splatters of lime-green margarita qualifies you as one.

"What'd she call you again? A thirsty trap?" Gramps speaks up.

I wave my hand, wishing I could drown my head in my margarita pitcher. It's big enough that my head would fit. "Nothing, it's fine! Lola, did you get anything fun for your birthday?" I smile forcefully at her sitting beside me. She seems to relish in the sudden attention, and her eyes go wide as she turns to face me, her hands reaching up to her earring.

"I got these beautiful flamingo earrings. I saw them in that little jewelry store in Duck, and someone remembered." She wiggles her head back and forth to demonstrate her larger-than-life pink earrings. Flamingos, set with little pink crystals. I look to Gramps, who blushes. I can't picture my practical grandpa walking into a store to buy those.

"Very cute. I like them." They're honestly weird as hell, but I could totally see myself buying them during a drunk, online shopping session.

Lola goes on about different birthdays she's had. Apparently, she swam with sharks in the Bahamas last year. *Maybe it's the margarita talking, but Lola is kind of a badass. Annoying, but badass.*

The conversation is interrupted by a band of middle-aged men setting up on the stage. We all turn their way as they introduce themselves and start playing a cover song. The moment the beats of the first song start strumming, Lola claps her hands together and gasps, exclaiming that this is her "favorite song ever." Though I have a feeling she would say that about any song just to get up and dance.

My eyes shift to her empty fruit cocktail, maraschino cherry eaten and all. Lola starts to sway, closing her eyes, and Gramps stands, extending his hand to pull her out of her seat. She acts bashful but springs over and loops her arm around his, pulling him to the dance floor. Well, to the middle of the deck where a few other happy vacationers have started swaying to the classic feel-good song.

The silence at the table is suddenly deafening now that it's just us two. So I study my empty margarita glass, debating whether I should pour a third drink. I could pull out my phone and pretend I have something important to check, but that would be a lie. I also hate when people pull out their phones at dinner. But Rowan's just sitting here, his arms resting across his chest, like he has no care in the world.

"How's your drink?" he questions, breaking the silence.

"Good. Would you like some?" I retort, craning my neck to look for the waitress. I want to ask for another glass, but I don't see her anywhere. Everything is a little spinny as I swivel back toward Rowan.

"I don't want any, but thank you."

"Okay," I say, dragging out the word dramatically. Now I really feel like a dumb drunk.

"Scarlett, did I offend you in some way?"

My face snaps back toward Rowan. His eyes glisten back at me with a small hint of disquiet on his face. "I don't care if you don't want to drink," I say more defensively than I mean to.

"No, not about that—" he starts, but I cut him off. It's a bad habit I need to break.

"Why would you ask that, then? What are you referring to?" My heart starts to race as I wait for his answer. I can't tell if he always seems so calculated or if I'm just that much of a mess.

"You just seem like you . . ." He searches for words, then lets out a huff of air, which blows hair off his forehead. "*Hate me* is the phrase I'm looking for."

My stomach drops. "I don't hate you," I reply calmly.

I don't hate him. I just don't *want* to trust him, even if he seems like the most trustworthy guy. They always seem like this at first.

"But I bother you. That much I can tell. If I did something wrong, or said something to offend you, I'd like to apologize." His confession catches me off guard. *They* don't usually say stuff like this.

"Why?"

"Why what?" He leans closer.

"Why do you care about apologizing to me? I'm not going to be here for very long, you know. It's not like you have an obligation to befriend me just because of Lola and my grandpa."

A feeling of self-hatred settles into my stomach as Rowan's brows furrow and shoulders slump ever so slightly.

"I don't like to leave bad blood on the table." He peels his gaze away from me.

"I simply don't see us being friends. We're different."

Different doesn't even begin to describe why I don't see us being friends.

"See? That wasn't so hard." His smile is undeservingly heart-melting. I can't imagine I'm the only one who's ever noticed that either.

"Happy now?" I smirk, stirring the ice in my glass, desperately wanting to refill it, but I decided to pace myself. Even if it's slightly too late.

He pauses a moment, biting his lip, then stares at me with intensity. "The thing is, most women who don't like me don't look at me like you look at me."

Heat rushes up my face. I'm glad I'm not holding my glass, or I would've dropped it.

"Wha—how do you mean? I am just *looking* at you. Get over yourself," I blurt out awkwardly.

"It's okay if I'm growing on you," he teases.

I scoff like a school-aged child. "You're growing on me for sure. Like a fungus on a tree." I know I'm being childish. And the margarita isn't helping.

"That's a beautiful image."

"Well, I'm just full of those," I reply, spinning in my seat to search for our waitress to flag down. I need water.

"Yes, actually, you are."

My heart skips a beat, and I pause, looking out over the restaurant before composing my face and turning toward him. His words don't have a playful, observant tone anymore. They're simply matter of fact. His words are clever. And I hate how I love it.

Lola and Gramps stumble back to the table. My eyes fall upon his hand on Lola's back, and he shrugs at me adorably. I smile back softly. Maybe in fifty years I can have something like that too. Fifty years should be enough time to get my shit together. I hope.

"Rowan James!" Lola drops her body into her seat dramatically.

Rowan's head snaps up, looking at his great aunt with a wide gaze.

"There is a beautiful young lady at the table with you. Ask her to dance already." She nudges me on the arm before winking at Gramps. If they planned this, I will need to have a talk with him later.

My heart drops into my stomach, and I scan the deck for a quick exit, but Rowan stands before I can find an excuse to go. He places his napkin on the table.

"May I?" He extends a hand, but I remain seated.

"Oh, you really don't have to do that. I can't dance," I say, excessively refusing his outstretched hand.

"All those years of dance lessons and you can't dance?" Gramps pipes up, calling my bluff.

Rowan winks at me slyly, probably intending to calm my nerves, but it makes me more uneasy. "One song," he says.

My eyes linger on his mouth a moment too long before I abruptly push my chair back in defeat.

"All right. Let's go, Casanova." I ignore his hand as I make my way to the crowded dance floor. Lola's eyes drill into the back of my head the entire walk to the center of the deck. "One song and it'll get her off my back."

He pulls me in closer, holding me firmly against him. Rowan's fingertips trace the small of my back as they come to rest on my hips, and I'm cocooned in his arms. There's no doubt about his strength, or his confidence, but the unexpected heat of his body against mine makes my mind go mushy for a moment.

The band plays a classic rock song, and it's mostly

married couples around us, with a few little girls swaying with their dads. It's like I fell through a portal; I haven't danced with a guy since homecoming in high school. I'm not sure the dancing at the music festivals I've been to count. No, this is different. It's . . . romantic? Or it would be if Rowan and I were a thing.

I slowly place my hands on his shoulders, and he adjusts his grip on my hips.

"She's persistent. She has that going for her," I say, trying to bring my heart back to a normal rhythm.

"That's one way of describing her. She's been overly concerned about me dating this summer. Now that she's back out there, she thinks I need to be too."

Now I laugh. Because that's ridiculous. Did she really think her straight-laced nephew would be a great match for me? If so, she doesn't know me very well.

"Well, that's stupid. Relationships usually suck more than not. Plus, she'll have to set her sights on someone else for you. I won't be staying here forever." I look over Rowan's shoulder at the dusky sky above the ocean. I'm a broken record. I know it. But the thoughts are flashing like a neon sign in my head.

"Hmm. Remind me again when you plan on leaving?" he asks.

"Next weekend was the original plan. For the most part, everything is planned out. It will only be two weeks since the heart attack, though." I pause, biting my lip. "It doesn't feel right to leave him so soon." I swallow hard the moment the words leave my mouth.

"What's Ray say?" Rowan asks as he spins me around, and I catch a glimpse of Gramps.

I snort. "What do you think? You see how opinionated he is. He thinks I should go, but he wouldn't be upset if I stayed either. He says he has all the help he needs." I raise my eyebrows at Rowan.

"And what do you want?"

"I don't know," I reply. A heaviness weighs on me.

"Right." He spins us around in the other direction. My favorite kind of sky is my new view—orange, red, and beautifully speckled with sinewy white clouds.

Rowan continues to lead us, and he's not half bad, surprisingly. But I won't tell him that.

"So what are you most excited to see?" Rowan moves the conversation along, causing me to swing my face around to his. It takes a moment to realize he is talking about my trip.

"The desert. The stars in the desert and a cactus ten times my size."

Rowan studies my face silently. His eyes trace my lips, then move to my eyes. "Well, I hope you love it. I hope it's everything you imagine it to be."

There's no sarcasm or sly rudeness in his voice. It's genuine. It's kind. If anything, there is sadness. I'd ask why, but I don't have time to unravel the inner workings of Rowan.

"Thanks . . . and I'm excited to run into the Pacific Ocean." I smile coyly at him.

"Why is that?" The song stops, and couples break apart, moving back to their tables. But Rowan stands there steady, waiting for my answer, like it's the only thing that matters.

"I grew up here . . . I know this place. I just want something new. The Pacific Ocean seemed really far away to me as a kid . . . and I've never been able to shake the dream of seeing it."

His head tilts slightly. I can tell he is thinking about my

answer. I'm sure he's letting it roll around in his mind, analyzing and trying to unlock the hidden meaning. He probably thinks if he can ask me enough questions and get enough answers, he will see who I am. He can't, though. That's not how it works with me.

I break my gaze away.

"Our food is here." I nod toward the table, and Rowan hesitates a moment before gently letting go of my hips. He follows me to the table, and I pinch my lips in, feeling like any second my brain will betray me and I'll blurt out something I'll regret.

Dinner goes on without a hitch—as in Gramps and Lola keep the conversation flowing and I get to sit there in silence, picking away at my calamari and polishing off my third margarita. But the sky starts to swirl as the clouds grow darker, and I know that's the tequila talking. The tequila is also making me steal glances at Rowan from across the table.

I think I've figured out why he gets under my skin. He is too calm—and kind. He asks questions that make me think, and he does everything right. It makes me uneasy, waiting for him to mess up.

The waitstaff brings Lola a piece of coconut cake with a candle in it and sings to her. I haven't been at a table where they did this since I turned fourteen and I made Gramps and Mimi promise me it was the last time they would humiliate me in public. But Lola is soaking it up, smiling at everyone around her, and when she blows out the candle, she closes her eyes to make a wish.

"What'd you wish for?" Gramps eggs her on like a little kid as Lola removes the yellow candle atop the cake. He always used to ask me when I was little and I'd get angry, telling him I can't tell or it won't come true. But Lola answers immediately.

"I wished for everyone at this table to find joy in their journey." She bats her long, fake eyelashes and grins gleefully. Gramps clamps his mouth shut and nods at her lovingly.

Find joy in your journey. I'm willing to bet that's also on a wooden sign, hanging up somewhere in her house.

Lola finishes her cake, and Gramps asks her to dance to one final song, which she obliges to without hesitation. Rowan and I both stand at the same time, unplanned.

"I'm just going to check out the beach. I'll be back in a few minutes." I smile, steadying myself on the back of my chair. Hats off to The Dancing Swordfish's bartender because they do not skimp on the liquor.

Rowan stands hesitantly, and Gramps interjects.

"Take him with you. It's getting dark on the beach." Gramps swings his head toward Rowan.

Did he seriously just tell a thirty-year-old man to babysit me? Rowan crosses his arms loosely, so I flash a tight-lipped grin at him and head toward the deck steps. One more moment and I'll say something unnecessarily rude about not needing a man to accompany me on a walk like I'm a frail little girl. I grip the handrail tightly, descending toward the water. His footsteps are close behind, and I fight the urge to quicken my pace and lose him. That would only make it worse, even if my margaritas tell me it will be fine.

As I reach the sand dunes, I kick off my wedges, undo my bun, letting it fall down my back, and ball up the fabric of my skirt as I walk toward the tide. The moon illuminates the beach enough to see where I'm going, and the string lights from the restaurant compete with the stars. The faint sound of the singer covering a Van Morrison song rings in my ears, but it's interrupted by the sound of steps in the sand behind me.

"For the record, I'm only down here because I wanted to walk. Not because your grandpa thinks you need to be supervised," Rowan says, throwing his hands up in surrender, stopping at the water's edge a few feet from me.

"It's fine. I needed to get away from the table anyway. It's just all . . . new to me."

"Them together?" Rowan says as he gently looks at me, resting his hands in his back pockets.

"Yeah," I reply softly. That, and being here on this island. And talking to a nice guy. It's disarming standing at the water with Rowan.

"It's all right. Civilian life is new for me." He nods toward the busy restaurant.

I don't know what to say. I'd heard about how hard it is for soldiers to return to civilian life, especially after a deployment. Especially after *multiple*. But I didn't want to sound ignorant and pretend I knew what he was dealing with, so instead I suggest what helps me drown out the noise.

"Want to walk?"

He nods and starts walking alongside me down the beach, his hands still in his pockets. I walk in the tide and let the warm water roll over my feet, which threatens to soak the hem of my dress. I love the predictability of the water. It's like a timetable. *One, two, three, four, five,* I count as it slowly recedes back into the massive ocean.

Then again, *One, two, three, four, five*, as it rolls back up the shore over my toes. It's always been steady.

"So you didn't always live here with Lola?" I start, continuing to stroll, looking at Rowan as I speak. "Where are you originally from?"

He runs a hand through his chestnut hair and knits his brows together. "I grew up in Massachusetts. But I joined the Air Force right out of high school and was stationed in South Carolina for a bit, Alaska, then Germany. Now, I'm here."

"Wow . . . that's a lot of places. So why the Outer Banks, then? I mean, I get it in the summer . . . but you can't be planning on staying here for good?"

"When I got out, I wasn't sure what I wanted to do. I needed a quiet place to just breathe for a while. I like the slow living here, and the company is turning out to be . . . nice."

I scoff, pausing to square off to him with hands tightly on my hips. "*Nice* is such a lazy word."

"What's wrong with *nice*?" He's lighthearted as he stops and faces me.

Without my shoes, Rowan stands almost a foot taller than me. I crane my face up to him.

"Nice is how you describe a well-behaved child or an experience at a restaurant. Nice is *boring*," I reply, my voice rising an octave as I explain.

"I didn't realize you were so passionate about semantics."

"I just hate being described as nice," I admit.

"Oh, so you think I was describing *you*?"

I'm grateful for the darkening sky, hiding my flushed face. "No! I think—" I start, but he takes a step closer to me, cutting me off.

"Okay, Scarlett. The company is . . . amicable."

I watch his lips move, soft and slow, as he speaks directly to me.

"The company is engaging . . . witty . . . tantalizing . . . magnetic . . . compelling . . . alluring . . ." His voice falls like honey from his lips, somehow growing more seductive with each word. My lips part without thought as his long list of synonyms for me hangs thick in the air between us. His body inches closer to mine with every syllable rolling off his tongue.

"Whatever is happening, it doesn't end well," I whisper breathily, fighting the fluttery feeling taking over my whole being.

Rowan's unphased, his body hovering a few inches from mine. "Tell me, what *is* happening?"

"I know guys like you. I've dated them. I know how this goes. So let me spare you a few weeks of your life," I confess, surprised by my own vulnerability.

"Tell me how it goes, then. I want to know." He runs his hand through his hair like my words don't scare him. I'm thrown off, but if Rowan James thinks he wants to know me, then fine. I'll tell him exactly who I am.

I step back and he comes fully into view.

"Okay. Here's how it goes." Out of habit, I cross my arms over my chest. "We hook up. You think you love me because I'm wild and free-spirited. I'm the rebellious girl you never got to fuck around with in high school, or college, because I was too busy giving all my attention to the bad boys, the ones who would knowingly destroy me. I sought them out like an animal to water. I craved self-destruction. And now it shows because my life is one giant trainwreck. So for a few weeks, you love it. You can at least tolerate it and look past it. You even say you

71

like how unpredictable I am. You love how quirky I am, how much fun I am, how hard I make you laugh. Hell, I probably will get along with your family because I'm a people pleaser and can get along with almost anyone if I *choose* to. It seems like it's all going great at first."

I pause to take a sharp breath and push my hair from one shoulder to the other. Rowan watches me as I continue.

"Until you realize, I don't really have a career. I bounce from job to job because I can't stand being told what to do and struggle to keep a real schedule, which means I never really have money. And my dog, she goes everywhere with me, which is so sweet at first, but then you think it's weird and annoying. You start to wonder why I don't have any real friends. I try to explain why, but in truth, I'm not really sure why I can't make friendships last. It's probably for the same reason I don't live in the same apartment for more than a few months at a time. Oh, and I blast music at ear-splitting volumes when I'm home alone because I don't like silence. You'll find that infuriating, I'm sure. So you'll try to fix me. You'll tell me you have a friend who owns a business and get me a job. *With benefits.* You'll try to introduce me to your friends' girlfriends so that my social circle can expand. You'll stop letting me order Thai takeout three times a week and tell me I need to buy clothes that make me look professional so your mom will approve of me. You'll tell me I'd look pretty as a brunette. You'll do everything you can to try to mold me into the girlfriend you need after you realize you've just been screwing the girl you only *thought* you wanted. And then, let's say this goes on for two months, six tops . . . Well, then you'll leave. You'll tell me you tried. You'll tell me you warned me. And you did. You tried, but then you gave up. And you're out. That's it. *That's* how this goes, Rowan."

I wipe the tear falling from my eye and take a deep breath to lessen the shaking of my body. Rowan stares at me with brows furrowed over pained eyes. With a tense jaw, he lets out a sigh too, shuffling his feet in the sand.

The air is heavy, and the tequila is too much. But I don't regret my words; he had to know. I'd be lying if I said I didn't think about it—what this might look like if I was brave, if I gave things a chance. But I only see the crash and burn. And the fire isn't worth the burn. It never has been.

The spiraling thoughts are hastily interrupted by Rowan's hands capturing the sides of my face, which sends a shock wave of calm down my body as he leans in, closing the gap between us. His lips brush mine, pausing, waiting for me to object.

Against my better judgment, I untangle my arms from my chest, grab onto his waist, and pull him into me. The warmth of his mouth turns my troubled mind into a puddle of liquid as he kisses me with need, and I kiss back with desire. Rowan entwines his fingers through my wind-blown hair, but I have to pull away after a minute. His pupils dilate as they meet mine, his mouth begging to be consumed. However, my intrusive thoughts return.

"I can't do this, Rowan," I whisper, pulling away quickly.

"Scar—" he starts, but I hold up my hand, and he pauses.

"I'm not staying here, Rowan. I'm not sure when, but soon . . . I-I think I'm going to take that trip out west, and I don't know what it means for me. I don't know when I'll be back." *If I do come back.*

73

"You keep saying that, you know. I know you're leaving, but . . ."

"*But what*, Rowan?"

"But you're still here. Right now."

I pinch my lips together. How did I let this happen? A fit of grunts and annoyances leave my mouth, and my fists grip tight to his shirt, pushing him one second and pulling him in the next. Logic stirs like oil in water in my heart. My vision blurs over from tears, and I let go of his shirt to lean down and loop my dress up in my hand.

"I'm sorry, Rowan," I reply, leaving him standing there at the water's edge as I run back to the restaurant, scooping up my shoes before going straight to Gramps's red truck. I lean my head against the passenger-side window, squeezing my eyes shut. My stomach clenches, threatening to dispel the liquor I downed, and the world starts to spin around me.

I open my eyes just a sliver to glance toward Lola and Gramps and am met with a chuckle. Gramps leans in to kiss Lola on the cheek, and they stand there embracing by Rowan's truck for a moment. Rolling to the other direction, I press my head into the truck again. Rowan's shadow makes its way over the dunes.

If I don't leave soon, I *will* crash and burn. And I'll end up dragging everyone down with me, ruining the perfect, safe bubble of happiness Lola, Gramps, and Rowan have here in this little town. If I'm going to crash and burn, I'm going to do it alone.

Chapter Eight

Some people drink. Some people smoke. Some open a browser on their phone and buy every item they see to make themselves feel better. But I walk. This morning, I wake up at six to walk. It's utterly unholy of me, but as the sun is just peaking over the horizon, I put on my tennis shoes and walk. First, I try to rouse Daisy to join me, but even with promises of beef jerky, she keeps her eyes shut and snuggles down deeper into bed.

So I leave her, skip down the front steps, and will my feet carry me where they want. They choose to go right, not left. I don't want to look at Rowan's truck in the driveway of the neighbor's house.

There are already a few people out, mostly runners. It's always the runners. Because why else get up with the sun if you're not going to be productive, right?

I walk all the way to the coffee shop in town. My legs burn, but my mind begins to feel clearer. The intoxicating smell of sugar invades my nose, which is torture, considering I've forgotten my wallet at home. My mouth salivates as I imagine what I would get. Iced coffee and a donut. A cake donut with powdered sugar to be exact. Because I believe icing belongs on cupcakes, and sprinkles only belong on ice cream. It's always been a powdered sugar donut for me, maple frosted for Gramps, and a French cruller for Mimi. I used to think you could tell a lot about a person by what donut they ordered. Or how they took their coffee. I wonder what Rowan would get. Probably a glazed donut and black coffee. Or no donut because he's a runner.

Damnit, this is why I went for a walk—to forget about Rowan.

So I keep walking—all the way to the pier. The sun's fully risen, meaning Gramps is already up. At the end of the pier, it's mostly fishermen, but I sit down anyway, allowing my legs to dangle over the edge, and let myself be swept away in thought.

But the only thought replaying in my head is the speech I gave Rowan. I *confessed* more to Rowan than I've been willing to admit to myself for a long time. And he pulled it out of me, like pulling a shell from the sand. There was no hesitation. My words came up so easily.

And the kiss . . . That *kiss.* Those kinds of kisses are dangerous. The ones you feel linger on your lips long after they're over. The ones you lay awake thinking about, your fingers gently caressing your mouth, wishing, *desiring* you could just kiss that person one more time *right now*. The kind of kiss that makes you say ridiculous things and do senseless stuff.

And that's why I walk. I'd walk all the way to California if I could right now.

❖❖ ⋅⋅◆⋅⋅ ❖❖

"Should I even ask?" Gramps cranes his neck to peer around the corner of the green recliner as I stand breathless in the doorway. Daisy perks up at my entrance, her lazy body curled around Gramps's slipper-covered feet.

"I needed fresh air. You already make coffee? I can make coffee. Maybe some toast and fruit?" My thoughts rapidly fire out of my mouth, and I pour coffee from the tin into the filter before Gramps has a chance to even reply. "You want jam on your toast?" I fire again, grabbing the loaf of bread from the bread box while knocking the paper towel holder off the counter.

My heart races so quickly that I have to grip the sink to regain balance. Scanning my wrists, I think about those fancy watches that track your sleep and heart rate and then report it to an app on your phone so you can see how morbidly sedentary you truly are. *Maybe I should buy one of those.*

"You got ants in your pants or something?" Gramps asks, scratching his head as he heads into the kitchen and shuffles past me.

"I figured I'm up, so why not? I feel like I haven't been the most helpful since I got here." I shove two pieces of bread into the toaster and aggressively slam the lever down. Thinking about how I told Rowan I will probably leave in a week twists my stomach into knots of guilt. How can I leave Gramps?

Gramps's brows knit together and he narrows his eyes at me. "I don't know where you get off saying things like this. You've been a joy to have around, Scarlett."

77

"But I came here to take care of you, and I don't know . . . I haven't done enough." I don't turn around to see his reaction as I pull two plates toward me and arrange the toast on them.

Almost seven years have passed since I left the nest. I've been back for holidays and the occasional weekend. I call, and I taught Gramps how to video chat, but it's never gotten easier. Every time I visit, I want to have more to show for my life. Every time I come back to see my only family, the only person who truly means the world to me, I feel like I've let him down. And now I'm here to help him after a medical emergency and I haven't even made it a week without getting myself into a situation that makes me want to run away again.

"Can I let you in on a secret, Scarlett?" Gramps's slippers pad along the tile floor, and he plops down at the kitchen table.

"Yes," I muster up, nervously awaiting his reply while carrying our plates to the table.

"I never needed you to be here," Gramps says matter-of-factly, eyes locked on mine.

He says it so easily, then takes a bite of jellied toast. It crunches, and I want to apologize for burning it. But he says nothing about it, and neither do I because my insides are knotted. I open my mouth, but he holds up his free hand while the other grips a slice of crunchy toast.

"I've been in this house—alone—for five years now. I can cook, I can clean—"

I stifle a laugh. Gramps can make a sandwich and wipe up spilled coffee. That's where his cooking and cleaning skills begin and end, but I don't want to squander his confidence.

"You've seen the way Lola feeds me. Rowan's even

gotten my groceries a few times. And all the folks from the parish check in on me if I'm not there on Fish Fry Fridays. Point is, kid, I've got a village here." He winks at me, and I raise my eyebrows in response.

"Okay . . . so you have a better social life than me." I sit back, stirring a spoonful of honey into my coffee.

"Well, you know what they say. Seventy-five is the new twenty-five." He takes a swig of coffee and chuckles to himself. He's not entirely wrong. The only reason I've been okay living hours from him is because he's always been independent, and until this heart attack, I never had the inkling he needed any help from me.

Gramps clamps a hand over his chest and his steel-blue gaze pierces my tired eyes. "I didn't *need* you here, Scarlett. I would've been fine. I have the money to hire a cleaning person, a nurse, anything I need, but I didn't want to. Because it was just a little heart attack."

I widen my eyes in response. I've told him before that no heart attack is *small*, but I can't protest his positive outlook.

"The good Lord blessed me with this life. And I am going to be just fine."

I slowly nod my head and glance at the cross hanging in the kitchen. "So if you didn't need me here, why did you ask me to come?"

He takes a deep breath and offers a small shrug. "I wanted to see you. I wanted to make sure you're okay. I wanted to spend time with my granddaughter before she leaves for her adventure."

My eyes get lost, unsure of how to feel. I thought I was coming here to take care of him, convinced he needed me. Gramps snaps his fingers, pulling his chair closer to the table, and my head rises to look at him.

"When I'm ninety-eight and someone needs to change my diaper, I trust you'll find a nice nursing home for me. One with a view of the ocean. Until then, I only *need* one thing from you. Well, three things actually." He winks and I swat his arm. When I was little, he used to joke that one day I'd have to hire a nurse to change his diapers when he got old, and I'd always dramatically gag and cover my ears.

"Okay, Gramps. What three things? And I'll remember that. Diaper changes with an ocean view, check." I take a bite of toast, registering how odd our conversations are. Mimi would snap the towel at us both for being *crass* while eating.

"One, don't worry about me. I would tell you if I truly needed assistance. Two, don't second-guess taking that trip. Life goes by in a flash. You've been dreaming about it for too long to just give up."

I nod.

"And three, come stay for Christmas. Every year, I want you here for Christmas." He smiles at me and tears prick the back of my eyes. I hate crying, especially in front of Gramps. I try to swallow them, but it's too late. He places a warm hand over mine.

"Deal. I promise." I mentally clock it. I won't miss Christmas—ever.

We finish breakfast as we fill each other in on our plans for the day. Nothing exciting from either of us, though he reminds me to drop the van off at Lu's Garage. I tell him I'll do that, though I know it will probably slip from my mind again.

Gramps's words sink in as I fill the dishwasher. He stands beside me, taking pills from the brightly labeled organizer Lola got him.

"One more thing, Scarlett Ray," Gramps turns to me as I wring the towel and gaze up at him, "don't let bitterness be your driver. Like Mimi used to say. I want to see you happy. I love you, kiddo."

I pause, masking my feelings with a soft smile. I let the towel drop onto the counter as he leaves the kitchen.

"I love you too, old man," I reply, meaning for it to reach him, but it comes out as a whisper.

It's only ten in the morning, yet somehow it feels like I've been awake for days.

Chapter Nine

O n Saturday, I spend the night on the sofa with my laptop glowing bright in front of me. Daisy settles in next to me, her wet nose blowing out warm air on my wrist while I browse online. Gramps has been out for an hour now, and the glow from the TV lights up the dark living room. It's quiet in the house, but my head is loud with his words. It seems like I've backed myself into a corner, telling Rowan I'm leaving for the trip, and now Gramps telling me he doesn't need me and wants me to go explore. Sometimes it feels like I came to this island for a planned intervention by Gramps and all who know him. Like they all got together and decided it's time to get Scarlett Ray to grow up, to make decisions.

So my browser is open. I'm revisiting the camping sites I booked months ago with Kellen and refreshing my memory of my plans. It's like looking at old photographs of myself.

That plan is temporarily killed the next morning when I go to start my van and it does nothing but sputter. Not the usual sputtering I've grown to find oddly comforting, but the kind that shakes the whole front end and concludes with a startling *pop*.

Defeated, I sit in the driver's seat when Rowan walks over, leaning into the half-open passenger-side window. "You need a hand there?" he asks, shielding his eyes from the blinding morning sun.

It's been two days since Lola's birthday. Two days since the kiss. And we haven't talked to or seen each other since. But Rowan's demeanor, as I tell him my van won't start, is as if it never happened. I can't decide if I'm grateful or hurt by it.

As Rowan pops the hood, Gramps saunters out of the house, peering down over the porch rail in his bathrobe with a coffee mug in hand.

"What's going on, Scar?" he hollers.

I shoot him a look, and throw my hands in the air, but Rowan intervenes. "Battery is dead. Probably among other things. I am going to try to jump it and take it down to Lu's if it starts."

"Wait, wait, no . . . ," I stammer defensively. I hate when people talk like I'm not even here.

"You have another plan?" Rowan asks, an edge to his voice. *So maybe he does remember Friday.* But still, he is here, helping me.

"No, not really, but I don't know. I just . . ." I come up empty. No real excuse why I shouldn't get it fixed. I suppose I wanted to handle this myself, but it's glaringly obvious I need Rowan at this point.

"Good." Rowan flashes a pearly smirk and tells me to take the keys out of the ignition.

I hesitate a moment, but do as he says, my eyes fluttering in undeserved annoyance. Gramps watches like a spectator at a baseball game while Rowan connects the cables to jump-start my van with his truck. His movement is effortless, like he's done this a million times. I watch as he readjusts his baseball cap to keep his hair from falling into his eyes. But I try not to stare as he leans over the hood of his truck, his shirt hanging from the pocket of his shorts. Evidently, it's suddenly too hot outside for him to stay clothed.

When he tells me to turn the van on and it starts, I have to bite my cheek to keep from smiling. Rowan smirks, though, while disconnecting the cables. He slams the vehicles' hoods shut, and I stay seated with my arms over my chest.

"Let's go," he says, gesturing to my van.

I gawk at him. *He fixes one little thing and thinks he now has authority over me?*

"Lu's is only open a few hours on Sunday. Better to get it there now before you need a tow." He adjusts my mirrors, and I want to swat his hand away, but I'm too flabbergasted to do anything but look vacantly at him. So I say nothing, just buckle up and lean out the window.

"Guess I'm going to Lu's!" I holler at Gramps, who gives me a thumbs-up, then disappears back into the house.

"I'll follow you there," Rowan says, pulling his shirt back on.

"That's not necessary. I'm a big girl," I reply, fully

aware of the irony. I couldn't have done this without him, and he knows it.

"You're not going to walk twenty miles home, are you?" he responds, tapping the roof of my car to make his point. Rowan raises his eyebrows and walks to his truck when I don't answer.

Touché.

I've never met Lu, but Gramps described him as an older man with short, white hair, which I find ironic, given he described himself and about eighty percent of the local population.

The door chimes and out walks a man who's shorter than me, with a smile on his face and a stitched name tag. I quickly wave, then slip my hand back into my pocket. He walks around to stand between Rowan and me.

"Hi, Lu. I'm Ray Peterson's granddaughter." I smile back at him, jabbing my thumb over my shoulder toward the big orange van. He eyes it up.

"Ahh, yes! Ray called a minute ago to tell me you're on your way. Tol' me you got a big ol' van, and he ain't lying, I see!" He throws his head back in laughter, his eyes crinkling a permanently suntanned face.

We follow him outside to look at the van.

"The battery is dying, I think," I say while Lu inspects it.

His bushy brows conceal his brown eyes as he squints at me in the sun. His eyes flick to Rowan, who's standing back silently watching with an amused look painted on his face.

"Well, ma'am, I'll check it out. Make sure we take care of that sputterin' I heard as you rolled in 'er and fix her all up for you." He winks at me and slaps the metal side, gesturing us to follow him into his office. It smells like motor oil, and you can't see an inch of the actual desktop, only piles of papers and keys.

"Will it be ready by Friday?" I cross my arms, nervously tapping my foot as he sifts through the drawer full of paper clips and coins.

"Yes, ma'am. Ray mentioned you got a trip planned. Well, unless there's something majorly wrong. Those things there are relics, ya know? They got unique parts. I'd have to order 'em from Raleigh if I don't got 'em here. Could be a month or two if that's the case."

His eyes meet my frantic expression and I gulp. If I don't leave Friday, I might chicken out of going altogether.

"But don't worry. I'll do my best. Could just be a battery." He winks at Rowan. "You two have a trip somewhere fun?"

I sputter like my car, and Rowan shakes his head slowly. "No, just me. And my dog," I speak softly.

Lu looks at both of us for a minute, licks his lips, and nods. "Uh-huh. 'Kay. Just give me a key, and you're good to go, Miss Peterson."

I wrestle the key off my key ring, which is obnoxiously full of glittery key chains, and hand it over to Lu. As I'm leaving the shop, Rowan opens the door of his truck for me, and I pause to look at him before climbing in. I'm about to say something snarky, but he rolls his head back and gestures into the vehicle, willing me to comply.

"Get used to it. I open doors for people," he retorts, walking around the front of the vehicle while I watch him through the windshield. He pulls himself in.

"For *people?* So you open car doors for everyone?" I pry, latching my seat belt and settling back into the seat.

Rowan pauses while he adjusts the air conditioning and peers at me out of the corner of his eye. Something about the way his jaw twitches when he looks at me sends tingles down my spine. And his car smells like him, woodsy and clean.

"Yeah. I open car doors for *people.* People I like. You have a problem with that, *Miss Peterson?*" he cracks at me, making me laugh at his imitation of Lu's deep, southern drawl. Rowan's smile creeps up the side of his face as he adjusts the radio and leans back in his seat.

"I like that," he says, his eyes lingering on me before reversing out onto the street.

"Like what?" I clutch my phone and key chain tightly against my lap.

Rowan's arm goes around the back of my seat, and he looks past me at oncoming cars. The closeness of his body near mine causes me to push myself further back into the seat.

"Your laugh. You have a nice laugh," he replies, looking at the road ahead as we roll down the narrow two-lane road.

"Oh." I fiddle with my hair and bite my cheek. "Thank you."

Rowan and I exchange quick smiles and go back to looking out the window. The radio host talks about the Fourth of July weekend coming up in two weeks. There's a big celebration in town with fireworks and food vendors. Families will flood the small towns and beaches. I bet Lola has a red, white, and blue outfit to sport and Gramps will go along with her to the town. I won't be celebrating. I wouldn't even if I did stay here. Ever since I got Daisy two years ago, I've had to stay home for the Fourth. She doesn't do well with fireworks.

I glance at Rowan's hands, steady on the black steering wheel. Mimi always said you could tell a lot about a man by their hands. Rowan's hands are big and strong. They're tanned from the summer sun and rough from the work he's been doing at Lola's. Honest hands. I wonder what he'll be doing on the Fourth of July. Will he be celebrating with everyone? Maybe he'll have a date to the festival.

"Where will you be on the Fourth?" Rowan asks, catching me off guard and breaking my train of thought. It's scary how easily I can fog over.

"Oh, um . . ." I try to think. If I leave on time, I'll be somewhere out west. Maybe I'll have made it to Colorado by then, or maybe I'll be up in the mountains. "I haven't figured it all out exactly. I have a few campgrounds booked here and there. I plan to just drive toward Southern California. So maybe I'll be in Colorado by then?" I reply quickly.

With one elbow on the door, Rowan props his head up. He glances at me and offers a small grin. "Colorado is beautiful this time of year. You'll love it." His raspy voice sounds far from here.

"What about you? Going to the pier to see the fireworks? I'm sure Lola won't let you say no to that," I joke, watching his smile turn into a straight line.

His eyes stay on the road, but the light in them dims. Rowan opens his mouth, shuts it, and opens it again before finally speaking. "No, uh . . . actually, I'll be home. Pretty boring. Probably watching a movie or something. I can't do fireworks." His eyebrows twitch together, and my mouth opens, forming an *O*, but no noise comes out.

"Well, you know what, I'll be joining you. In Colorado, of course. Daisy gets really scared, so usually I wrap her in a blanket, and we veg out and watch movies. We always eat cookout food at home, and I have this red, white, and blue bandanna for her. It's actually kind of nice to be low-key," I admit, and Rowan cracks a smile—a genuine smile—and laughs.

"That sounds ideal right there. Daisy is a lucky girl." He rubs his mouth with his hand, and I peel my eyes away.

I push away the thought of him being alone. It doesn't matter that I barely know him. It still sucks to think he'll be by himself. If I was here, would we chill together and watch movies? Would I hold Daisy in one arm while the other side of me is tucked into Rowan's shoulder? I shouldn't let myself wonder about these things. Letting butterflies take up permanent residency in my stomach when I can't even admit I like Rowan is idiotic of me.

The feeling dissipates as we pull into Lola's driveway and I notice someone sitting on Gramps's front steps.

My throat tightens. The seat belt suddenly feels restrictive against my chest. I want to shout at Rowan to gun it out of here and take me anywhere but *here*. But I can't. I just keep staring at her.

Chapter Ten

I never thought I would be able to recognize her in a crowd of people. Her face was stuck in my mind like it was when I was six, but time's passed. People change.

But *she* didn't change. She was still willowy with sandy hair rippling down her back. It's just a little thinner and teased up a little higher now. Her cheekbones jut out from under black sunglasses. I would know her anywhere.

"Scarlett, you okay?" Rowan's voice breaks through my trance.

My body leans forward as if I've lost all control of it. He traces my line of sight back to the woman when I don't answer right away. She's digging through her purse on the steps.

His hand reaches out, covering my knee lightly. "Do you know her?" Concern coats his voice, causing a lump to form in my tight throat.

I swallow hard, not ready to divulge that intimate part

of my past. The topic of my mom hasn't come up naturally yet, and it's never been something I mention freely. I nod at him reassuringly. "I better go. Thanks for the ride and for everything else," I mutter.

He removes his hand as I slide out of the truck. His gaze follows me around the truck as I march straight toward Gramps's house, straight toward her. You could convince me time was standing still as I walk across the seemingly never-ending stretch of land. With every step, adrenaline builds in my body.

My feet come to a dragging stop at the bottom step. I glance back toward Lola's house. Rowan watches with an apprehensive gaze, but I wave, and he waves back before slowly making his way inside.

Gramps's truck is gone. He told me what he was doing this morning, but the conversation is a bit fuzzy. Did he say he was getting lunch with a friend? I don't know now.

Then my eyes meet hers. A perfectly manicured hand shields her blue eyes from the sun, and the glittering diamond on her ring finger catches a ray. My stomach flips like I'm being tossed around under water.

"Mom?" I mutter somewhere between a question and a statement. The sun beats down on the back of my neck, and a gentle breeze wraps around my body like a scarf, pushing strands of faded pink hair into my eyes. I can't move a muscle. I simply stare at her. In disbelief. In shock. Anger begins to boil in the pit of my stomach.

Her tight lips twitch at the sound of my voice. It's not enough to call it a smile, but it's her only response. "Hi, Scarlett," she replies sheepishly, her accent thicker than I remember. Though, I'm not sure if I ever really remembered her correctly. She picks up her bag and stands straight, crossing her arms while she glances left and right.

It dawns on me in that moment how different she is. She's not the same woman who stood on the church steps nineteen years ago. That person looked like a girl with lost eyes and clothes too big for her. She wore whatever Mimi made her or what she could afford from the thrift store. I remember thrifting with Mom. She turned it into a game, making me believe we were on a secret treasure hunt.

This woman, standing on the steps in front of me, somehow seems ten feet taller. Her designer purse probably costs more than my van, and the thin, gold chain around her neck holds a single pearl, gleaming in the sunshine. She moves a hand to her neck, clutching the necklace when she notices me looking at it.

"Can we talk?" she asks, her voice scratchy, eyebrows knitted together.

The gentlest breeze could knock me over right now. But I swallow, trying to wet my dry mouth, as if that would help me find the words to say in this situation.

"About what?" I murmur back, looking past her to the door.

Daisy's sweet face peers out the living room window at me. Her ears perk up when we make eye contact, then the brown spot around her eyes crinkles with concern as she looks intensely at me. Daisy always knows when I need her.

My mother's head slowly turns, following my gaze. She cracks a small smile after seeing Daisy in the window. "Is that your dog, Scarlett?" she asks, like she is speaking to a young child. I guess the last time she spoke to me, I was a young child. My name sounds foreign on her tongue, like she hasn't said it in a long time.

I walk swiftly by her, up onto the porch, and jam my key into the lock.

"Scarlett, please. I just need to say a few things. Can I *please* come in?" she pleads, so I whip around to look at her. I want to tell her to go, but I realize there is no car. I wonder if she walked here, though that seems unlikely considering the pristine, leather wedge sandals she has on.

Flustered, I turn back to finish unlocking the door, and the sound of Daisy pushing her snout into the other side of the door makes the knots in my stomach tighter. The sound of her nails scraping on the door is loud. I want to squeeze into the house and lock the door behind me.

"Scarlett . . . ," she pleads again more softly.

I take a deep breath. I have nothing I want to say to her. Now that she is here in front of me, the questions I had don't seem to matter anymore.

"Five minutes, then you need to leave," I reply curtly, pushing the door open and walking into the foyer.

My first instinct as I walk into Gramps's home is to protect him. After all this time, I don't want to imagine what seeing her would do to him. She has to be gone before he gets back. Daisy nuzzles my hand as I walk in. I'm still feeling floaty as I kneel down to kiss her head.

The screen door creaks behind me, but I don't pause to welcome her. Instead, I trail into the kitchen. Daisy looks to me, then my mom, undecided if she should greet the stranger. Her sweetness wins out, and she scampers toward her, wiggling with excitement. I clutch the fridge door, whipping it open to pour myself a glass of iced tea, and see my mom standing in the kitchen when I shut the door. She clutches her purse to her chest while Daisy carefully inspects every inch of her shoes.

"You finally got a dog," she observes, not smiling or petting Daisy. She didn't let me get a dog when I was young, but the week after she left, Mimi brought home an entire litter of foster puppies, and my seven-year-old heart swelled with love. Ever since, there hasn't been a day without a dog.

"What are you doing here?" I snap, not having time for small talk.

Her face falls a little, but she pulls out a kitchen chair and sits down like it's her table, as if she sits here every morning with her family.

Daisy finally gives up trying to get any love from her and sits next to me in defeat, leaning her solid mass into my legs. I continue to stand stiffly, my hip grounded by the hard counter behind me.

"I know this is unexpected, and I know this isn't easy, Scarlett . . . but—" she starts, but I cross my arms, the anger boiling over in me as I sputter out my thoughts without filter.

"Unexpected? A flat tire is unexpected. My mother showing up out of the blue after nineteen years, that's not unexpected. That's fucking insane!"

She flinches as my forceful outburst awakens the silent house. Her widened eyes look away from me, and her mouth opens and closes without a sound.

"What gives you the right to show up at Gramps's house a week after his heart attack? Or five years after Mimi's death? Hmm?" I egg on, feeling my heart push against my rib cage. "When you left us, you gave up the right to show your face here. You gave up the right to ever enter our home again. Don't you dare start with 'This isn't easy' when you grew up with a mother like Mimi, who was a saint! And *I* grew up wondering why the hell my mom left me on a random Wednesday morning!" I've evolved to a scream, not even noticing until I stop talking that there's a waterfall of tears gushing from my eyes.

Her face falls completely flat, eyes crestfallen on the kitchen table. I don't feel an ounce of remorse because nothing I'm saying is a lie.

"I am *sorry*, Scarlett Ray," she says, lifting her head to me. Her eyes are the same deep blue as Gramps and mine. "I was so young when I had you. I had no idea what I was even doing. I was depressed and scared, and I knew you deserved better. When I saw a way out, I took it. I never thought my decisions would cause you so much pain," she says, and her eyes begin to well with tears.

I heard her excuse, but I can't make sense of it. It doesn't add up. She wasn't perfect back then by any means, but I loved her. But now I wonder if maybe I just wanted to remember her that way. To protect myself.

"You were twenty-five when you left me. Are you aware that's how old I am now?" I ask, and she looks at me with deafening silence. "We all get scared and depressed and make bad choices when we're young. You can't run from it. You get yourself together, and you return. And you be the fucking mother you were supposed to be. Running away isn't a *way out*. Trust me, I know." My legs tremble and my head feels light.

Daisy licks my leg, so I kneel down to hug her, needing something to bring me back down. Even if the world dealt me every bad card in the deck, I wouldn't leave Daisy. So how could this woman across from me leave her own child?

I glance at her, but she isn't looking at me. Our looks are the only thing we have in common. Nothing inside her resembles me.

"April twenty-ninth," she says, pushing her blonde hair back from her eyes and sniffling. Her tears already evaporated, and the stoic look has returned to her face.

"What?" I narrow my eyes in response, still hugging Daisy on the floor of the kitchen. The wood floor is sticky on my bare legs, but I'm frozen here.

"That's your birthday. And for the last nineteen years, I've sent you a card. I've never forgotten." Her words feel like a tidal wave crashing down on me. Dread hits me in the core as I struggle to form sounds.

She tilts her head to the side. "Have you never gotten a card? I know Dad never cashed the check, but I thought he would *at least* give you the card." She peers down at me like I should know what she's saying, like I'm an ignorant little kid.

"I have no idea what you're talking about." I pronounce every syllable, vying to find clarity in this conversation. Pulling myself up off the floor, I shakily tap a sip of iced tea, which is hard to swallow given the tightness in my throat.

"Will he be back soon? I . . . I didn't know about the heart attack."

I bite my tongue to keep myself from screaming, *Of course, you didn't know! You know nothing about this family!*

"I don't know when he'll be back, but I do know you need to be long gone before he gets here." I clutch the cold glass to my chest before taking a deep breath. "His heart can't handle *this*, and I'm not going to lose the last person I have."

Her shoulders shudder with the impact of my words. *I hope they sting.*

"I'm sorry. I will go . . . but please give this to him." She

96

pulls out a card with "Ray" written on the envelope. She holds it out toward me, but I keep my arms to my chest, and after a moment, she sets it on the table in defeat.

"And this is for you." She pulls out a thick manila envelope with "Scarlett" scribbled on it. She sets it down on the table gingerly and glances at me before pushing back her chair to stand. I watch in silence as she smooths her dress down and walks to the front door with her head held high.

She can't disappear that easily. There's one more question I need answered.

"Why now? How did you know I was here?" I ask loudly, causing her to pause. I lean against the kitchen doorframe, and she stands with one foot out the front door. Hesitant, she avoids eye contact.

"I'm here with my family on vacation. In Nags Head. I didn't know you'd be here too."

I can't even nod in response. I stare blankly as she walks out the door, down the steps, and into an expensive-looking SUV waiting for her on the street. She drives away, and I'm still standing here. A million seconds go by, and I'm still standing here, staring out the screen door she left open. At least when she left the first time, I didn't have to watch her walk away.

Another family. She left Gramps, Mimi, and me to get *better.* To find herself. And she did. *With another family.* Did she start over? With a rich man who could give her the world? Does she have more kids who she adores? Does she take them treasure hunting, or do they have all the things money can buy?

My body succumbs to the weight of this day, and I slide down the wall next to the front door, leaning my head back and closing my eyes. Daisy wanders over to sniff me, offering a few wet kisses. My head's heavy against the wall, but no tears come. Only a pit in my stomach, creeping its way into my chest. I sense the cavity reopening in my heart, the one I thought had closed a long time ago. With my chin on my knees, I peer around the quiet house. The stillness makes me evidently aware of how alone I am right now. How I wish Mimi was here. She'd know what to say to make this better. She'd offer her comforting love that would take the pain away.

But she isn't here. And I can't sit here any longer, even if I want to sit until I disappear. So I numbly pull myself up, and my shaky legs carry me to the bathroom. Dousing my face with cold water, I try to regain awareness of my surroundings. My fingers dig into the sink's edge, and I make eye contact with myself in the mirror. I appear more tired than I expected, and I have to stare at my reflection for what seems like an eternity just to remember who I am.

Because right now, I am as small as the little girl who was left all those years ago.

"Scarlett? I'm home!" Gramps's voice rings through the hallways.

He wanders around the house, searching for me. I say nothing until he knocks on my ajar bedroom door. My shoes remain on as I lay on the bed, watching the ceiling fan go round and round.

"You feeling okay? The front door was left wide open." I glance over to watch him remove his cap and ruffle his flattened hair. My stomach clenches as he smiles at me.

"How was Lu?"

I prop myself up on my elbows, my puffy red eyes meeting his. "Why didn't you tell me about the birthday cards?" I ask, cutting to the chase.

Gramps looks away, and I stiffen as a look washes over him I've never seen. Panic, fear, reality? I know *he knows* what I'm talking about.

"What cards—" he starts, but I cut him off.

"*The* cards. The ones . . . Mom sent." *Mom* never felt natural on my tongue.

His eyes fall to the ground, and his mouth quivers as he reaches for the dresser to grip on to. "How did you . . .," he begins to ask quietly, and I spring off the bed in response.

I'm torn between wanting to protect Gramps from the fact that his only daughter was here in his house just hours ago and simultaneously crumbling inside.

"It doesn't matter how I know. Just tell me if it's true. Tell me why," I plead with him.

"We wanted to protect you." His voice comes out like a low rumble, and it shatters me.

Mimi *and* him, of course. Both of them, all these years. They must've stashed the cards away. Somewhere.

"Protect me from what? All this time . . . you let me believe my own mother forgot about me?" I wipe my eyes, unsure how there is anything left in me to spill out.

"Scarlett, she was *not* coming back. A birthday card would've just confused you. You were so young." Hurt flashes in his eyes, and pain tinges his voice. Hurting him was never my intention, but I can't take anymore.

I lunge toward the nightstand, grabbing my key ring, only to remember I don't have a car right now.

"Scarlett," Gramps warns, but I vigorously shake my

head, not daring to look at him.

"I need space. And air," I say and shimmy past his still body in the doorway, grabbing my beach bag and heading straight out the front door. I can't take Daisy with me right now. But I'll be back. I will *always* come back.

The bicycle tires screech against the hot pavement as I peddle as fast as my trembling legs will allow. My old beach cruiser bike from high school can barely keep up. Five miles later, my limbs are on fire, but it's a welcome distraction from my spiraling train of thought. And I know there's only one way to calm it.

I drop my bike with the rest at the public beach entrance, change into my swimsuit in a dash, and march straight onto the sand, lazily dropping my stuff in a messy heap. I don't care how swollen my eyes are, how messy my pink hair is, or the fact that my rings are still stacked on my fingers as I dip into the water.

The foamy waves push back as I wade deeper. I fight to stand back up and keep walking, my eyes trained on the horizon. The cold shocks me when the water hits my chest, but I keep moving until I can no longer feel the sandy bottom beneath my feet.

And then I go under.

Chapter Eleven

When I was younger, Mimi used to take me to Wrightsville Beach outside of Wilmington to swim. All summer long, she would recline in her striped folding chair with a library book in hand, and I'd swim. Sometimes I'd make friends with other kids on the beach, and sometimes Gramps would join Mimi and me. Other times it would be me alone. Fearlessness made me a strong swimmer—that, and ignorance.

As I float, my eyes are closed to the sun. My memory propels me back to being seven years old, with long and messy hair floating around me as I bobbed in the waves, always holding tight onto my snorkel. With every fiber of my being, I'd hoped a mermaid would find me out there. Because at seven years old, it only made sense they'd invite me to live with them in the deep ocean. I had my response memorized for such occasions too: I'd tell them "no" because my Mimi would worry about me and I'd miss my dogs. For a while, too, I was convinced my mom ran away to be with them. It was what I'd told myself when I was sad about her leaving. Because if she was with them, then at least she'd be happy.

The memory disappears, and I focus on the hypnotic murmuring of the deep water. I swim out further, losing sight of the families on the beach. The kids' screams fade as the waves rush to their feet. Moms are doting on their children, and I twirl my body back toward the empty horizon.

I wish the ocean could swallow me and spit me out somewhere else. I can't stay out here forever, floating in this endless sea, but the alternative of going back to shore sounds impossible too.

So for now, I'll just drift.

After a while, my muscles grow more tired than my stubborn mind, and I don't fight the waves as they carry me to the shore. My body is heavy with dripping water as I trudge back to my heap of possessions. They're still sitting there in a chaotic sand-covered pile.

Shaking out the faded beach towel, I lay down and let the sun evaporate the salty water from my skin. The lulling of the waves crashing in and the solidness of the packed sand beneath me bring me some comfort. As much comfort as I can hope for in this fucked-up situation.

However, I can't shake the imagery playing in my mind when I shut my eyes. The image of nineteen birthday cards haunts me, and I wonder where they are. Does Gramps still have them? If he does, do I truthfully even care what they say?

Reading them would be like opening my life's time capsule, one I didn't even know existed until mere hours ago. Among the miscellaneous boxes of collected junk in my van, somewhere I have a box of keepsakes. It contains every birthday and Christmas card I've ever received from Mimi and Gramps. I could never will myself to throw them out, not even the ripped envelopes they came in, knowing they picked each one specially for me. But there's no room in that keepsake box for Mom's cards. They would be intruders. Disruptors to the story I've believed my whole life.

I roll heavily onto my stomach, propping myself up on my elbows. While I scan the rows of houses lining the beach, I wonder which one she's in. Her and her *family*. Does she take her kids to the beach to swim and play? Does she get in the water with them and collect shells for necklaces like she did with me? I can't imagine the woman sitting in Gramps's kitchen doing any of that. Or maybe her cold demeanor was reserved only for me.

However, the notion that somewhere nearby is the family she chose over *us* makes my stomach flip, filling me with unease. And just like that, nothing about this beach brings me peace anymore.

There's only a bit of moisture left in my hair, so I twist it up and push my pink sunglasses up the bridge of my nose. I don't know where I'm going next, but I can't sit on this beach surrounded by happy-go-lucky people any longer.

The leather seat is scalding hot by the time I return to my bike, but I hop on anyway, making my quick escape. I slow down as I hit the main drag in town. If I go right, I'll be back at Gramps's house in minutes. My arms jolt left at the last second, and I find myself in front of the hardware store instead.

While waiting to cross, I scan the parking lot and see Rowan's black truck. The light turns green, but I don't move. Rowan exits the store, holding a heavy-looking bag. His arms flex around it, and he glances my way. I feel pulled in by his presence and slowly walk my bike over to him.

"Hey! You coming back from the beach?" he asks sarcastically.

"What gave it away?" I reply dryly, feeling awkwardly disheveled after letting the ocean and sun beat me up the last few hours.

"If you're heading home, I can give you a ride." He nods toward his truck, and without thought, I shake my head.

"No, I'm not . . . I'm just heading—" I look around in all directions, frantically pointing straight ahead. "—that way."

Rowan glances the way of my finger. "And what's that way?"

"That way is *not* home. I can't go home yet."

He looks down at his wrist, his watch face lighting up. Then back at me. "You hungry?"

My stomach growls in response, begging me to say yes. "I don't have anything on me but beach stuff actually," I reply, my feet creeping up to the pedals, ready to push off and ride away.

In some way, I can't believe how rattled seeing my mother made me, and yet I feel like if I become completely undone it would also be warranted. Nothing could've prepared me for any of this. But losing my cool in front of Rowan is the last thing I want. Been there, done that.

"It's my treat," Rowan interjects, and I hesitate, chewing my lip, but he continues. "Please, it's just a meal. And I'm hungry as hell." He drags out the last word, and I can't help but crack a smile.

"Okay, fine. But I'm getting you back." I walk my bike next to him as we head toward his truck. He grabs the bike from me, effortlessly tossing it into the back. Rowan also opens the door for me, and I don't have a wise-ass comment this time. He simply nods as I slide in.

"What are you in the mood for?" He waits patiently for me to answer. He must not have dated much. Doesn't he know this is a pointless question to ask a hungry woman?

"Um . . . one, somewhere I don't have to see people. Two, someplace that serves alcohol preferably," I rattle off, glancing out the window at the passing buildings. "Maybe pizza. Oh, breadsticks sound good too." I face him, grinning coyly. "But you can choose, Rowan. I'm not picky," I add.

Rowan throws his head back and lets out a quick laugh. He opens the center console, placing his aviators in a felt-lined holder, a row of change neatly stacked beside it. His car is immaculately clean. Everything has a place. There's a place for everything in his life. Well, almost *everything*.

"So it sounds like you *do* know what you want. But I actually have an idea too . . . if you trust me?"

I narrow my eyes at him. I hate *ideas*.

"I'm not sure . . . ," I respond slowly, but he smirks, turning the truck sharply into a passing pizza joint.

"I'm going to grab the food, and you run across the street to grab the drinks." He pulls a twenty out of his wallet and hands it to me.

I snatch it and smile, heat pulling on my core. "Okay," I reply. This simple action overwhelms me, and tears well

105

in my eyes, but not before I exit the truck.

Rowan pauses at the pizza shop door and yells out as I'm about to cross the street. "Pepperoni, cheese, veggie? What do you want?"

"Everything. I want it all!" I answer truthfully, and he chuckles, ducking into the shop.

Twenty minutes later, we pull into an empty park, and Rowan backs the truck up to the water's edge. It's a rundown park that no one comes to anymore, unless you're a sixteen-year-old looking for a place to hook up. But then again, I did tell Rowan I didn't want to see or talk to anything, and he delivered.

I already hear the sound of the night bugs starting their symphony as we arrive. Once we're parked, I reach to open the cardboard lid of the hot pizza, but Rowan snatches the box just out of my reach.

"Not so fast. We have to do this the right way."

I scrunch up my face. "The *right* way? We're about to eat pizza and open a gas-station six-pack. Is there a wrong way?" I attempt to grab the box again, but he nudges my hand away, making me groan. He's awfully complicated for such a simple guy.

"Grab the beer and follow me," he instructs, piquing my curiosity, so I do as he says.

We walk around to the back, and Rowan pulls a few blankets from the back seat, padding the dusty truck-bed interior. He makes a show of it, smoothing it down perfectly, like he's making a military bed. Rowan hops up and set the pizza down. Standing there, I'm baffled by this strange but devilishly handsome man. My heart races like crazy for the umpteenth time today. But the cause is welcome this time.

I latch onto his arm, and he pulls me up swiftly. We sit across from each other, and Rowan finally opens the pizza. A genuine chuckle escapes from my mouth as he continues the show, popping open two beers and handing me one like we're at some five-star restaurant.

"So this is the proper way, huh?" I joke.

"Yes, it is," he replies, sipping the top of his beer while keeping his gaze on mine.

I break my eyes away and grab a hot slice of pizza, careful not to inhale the whole thing. We eat in silence for a moment before I let my thoughts slip out. "Thank you for this." I don't look at him as I express my gratitude, but I see him nod. "I really didn't want to go home yet." I exhale.

"I didn't really want to go home either," he replies.

"Oh." His statement catches me off guard. "Why's that?"

"I guess I was hoping I'd run into you."

"Oh!" I reply, a little too loudly. It's becoming clear I only have two modes when I'm around Rowan James: an awkward girl who rambles or speechless. I wonder if I'll ever manage something in-between.

He must sense my awkwardness, or unwillingness, to dive into that subject matter, and I'm grateful when he switches the subject.

"Does your not wanting to go back have anything to do with the woman sitting on the steps this morning?"

"Correct." I nod sharply.

"And I also get the sense you don't really want to talk about it yet."

"Correct again. You're on a roll, Rowan James!" I joke, winking while taking another sip of beer.

"Fair enough. We can just sit here, eat, and talk about something else," he says, slowly taking another bite of crust.

"Okay, tell me something. Um . . . something about yourself I don't already know," I say.

"Hmm . . . like a secret?" He furrows his brow.

"Yes!" I inch closer, amused at how ruffled my suggestion made him. I wipe my hands on a napkin and pause to watch him fiddle with the buttons on his Henley shirt, biting his lip. His eyes linger on the clouds while he ponders my question.

"Okay. I don't swim in the ocean," he confesses, letting out a little breath.

I scrunch my face in disbelief. "What? Like you've never swam in the ocean . . . *ever*?"

He shrugs, grabbing another slice of pizza, avoiding eye contact. "I don't like swimming if I can't see my feet."

"So let me get this right . . ." I smile, and he tilts his head, raising his eyebrows at me as I reiterate his confession. "You have been deployed overseas twice, but you draw the line at swimming in the ocean. Is it the sharks?" I tease, not letting him off the hook for this one. I've found a flaw in this perfect man.

He leans forwards until his face is inches from mine. His smoldering eyes make my lungs suddenly forget how to function. Slowly, he replies, "I did *not* say I'm afraid of sharks."

"Right, sure. Your secret is safe with me," I tease back, and his intense stares wavers, crinkled by a smile. I never knew a single look from someone could make me feel so exposed.

"We can't all be as fearless as you, Scarlett," Rowan leans back on the cab wall, placing a perfectly sculpted arm on the side.

I let out a sarcastic chuckle. He might be near perfect, but he isn't perceptive. Fearless is the last word I'd use to describe myself. Maybe reckless. But fear . . . There are plenty of things I fear.

"I have you fooled, then. I'm far from that. I simply like the weightlessness of the ocean. I always have. Floating in water is the only thing that calms me down sometimes." I pop open another beer, hoping I didn't overshare again. "You should try it sometime. Next time you're feeling brave, *soldier*, you can come with me and I'll show you how to do it."

I tilt my beer to him, and he sits there, eyes trained on me.

"What?" I utter, my hand flying to my face as his eyes stay on me. "Shit, is there food on my face?"

Rowan laughs softly, shaking his head at me under his thick eyelashes. He rubs the back of his neck. "I just . . . I like this side of you."

"This side?" I spit back at him. "I'm a hot mess with swollen eyes from crying, who's hard to love, with an attitude problem. According to my ex, that is. Oh, and I forgot, I have a knack for making poor decisions," I awkwardly reply, giving him a lame thumbs-up to break the tension, but he doesn't laugh. Instead he remains still, his eyes boring into me.

"I was going to say real, unguarded . . . maybe even adorable."

Heat rises up my body, and I throw my head back to finish the beer before looking at Rowan again. The truck cab feels small suddenly.

Neither of us says anything. The words hang in the air until I speak what's heavy on my heart. "Rowan, what are we doing here?"

"We're enjoying dinner together." He looks at me with such emotion it feels like it could break me.

"But why are you doing this? You're being so nice to me, and I've been . . ."

Rowan pushes the pizza box aside and crawls across the truck bed to sit next to me. "I know whatever you're going through isn't easy, Scar."

This time, I allow him to use my nickname. It comes out of his mouth like honey, and I want to ask him to say it again, but he keeps going.

"You've asked me why I'm here, so I'll tell you," he says, his eyebrows furrowing with sincerity.

"Okay," I barely whisper.

"When I joined the military, my family stopped talking to me. My parents were outraged I chose to enlist instead of following in my father's footsteps and attending his ivy league alma mater. I had the grades to get in, but I wanted something else for myself. I wasn't a scholar like the rest of them, and I let them down. Lola isn't like them, though. She's had my back since day one. She took me in when my family cut me out. It's been nearly twelve years, and they still barely speak to me. So that's why I'm here. I'm figuring it out too." He lets out a dramatic puff of air and runs his fingers through his hair. "We aren't that different, you know?"

"I'm so sorry, Rowan." Blood rushes to my cheeks as a bout of emotions flood me. I grab his arm, and he offers a tight-lipped smile to say it's okay.

"Don't be sorry. Be grateful. You have people who look out for you and love you."

"I know . . . and I wouldn't trade him for the world," I reply, and we pause, a comfortable silence falling over us. Then I continue my train of thought. "I don't know what I'm doing here either. I thought my grandpa needed me, but now I'm realizing maybe I had it wrong. Maybe I needed him."

"It's okay to let people take care of you," he states sternly, taking my hand in his. A gesture so small, but so powerful.

"Is that what you're trying to do? Take care of me?" Heat rises in my chest and simmers just as fast as Rowan's other hand feathers against the side of my face, coming to rest on the back of my neck. He cradles my head in his hand, and the tension between us is too much. One more word, one more breath, one more look, and I will burst.

"If you'd only let me," he gravelly whispers back.

There it is, the final raindrop in the barrel that makes it spill over.

My lips crash into his, and my hands search for his body the moment his tongue parts my lips. I can't get close enough quick enough, and Rowan doesn't pull away. Instead, he leans back carefully, shifting our bodies until I'm resting on top of his, our breathing ragged but in sync. We kiss slowly, then roughly, ebb and flow, grabbing each other like it's somehow our first and last time. I push away every ounce of self-loathing I've bottled up and let myself melt into his touch. I'm sick of fighting, of denying. Right here, right now, I want this. Whatever this is. My fingers slip from his neck to his pants, finding the clasp over the hardness forming below them.

"Scar . . . are you sure?" His breath is ragged, and a familiar desire in those beautiful eyes searches for my answer. There is no one but us in the moment. No betrayal, no secrets, no wondering. Just Rowan and me.

"This is me *letting* you take care of me," I whisper breathily, and Rowan closes the gap, pulling me feverishly around him as he flips me onto my back, covering me with himself. I let him be my shelter.

There are no more words spoken between us. Kisses butterfly down my neck to my collarbone, and the sound of our clothes being shed. Layers come off until nothing sits between us. I nod against his mouth, begging him to give me everything, and he does. For a while, I forget about the mess, and I'm just Scarlett. In the moments Rowan holds me, treating my body like it's the most precious thing, I'm not my story.

Rowan isn't quick to move after, but instead pulls me into his arms while we lay there, looking at the dusky evening sky. The water in the Sound is still, mimicking my heart.

"Scarlett?"

"Hmm?" I hum, not wanting to break this moment.

"You're not hard to love."

Those words sink into my skin and encase me. I don't move, just pull Rowan a little closer and let myself feel safe. I watch my arm move up and down as its draped across Rowan's abdomen. The ink of the compass tattoo pulls me back to reality. My reality.

Enjoy this Scar. It's fleeting.

Chapter Twelve

Rowan holds me tight in the bed of his truck, and we look out at the Sound together for what seems like forever. Or maybe I'm tricking my mind into thinking it's forever because I don't want it to end.

I can't stay here with him, though. Despite my anger with Gramps, I still love him fiercely. Perhaps that's my downfall, or maybe that's how it is with the man who raised you. Either way, he is all I have left. And Daisy is probably wondering when her mother is going to return.

Rowan's rhythmic breathing pulls me from my thoughts. His embrace feels natural. I want to close my eyes, ignore my reality, and stay here in the peaceful safety of a kind man's arms, but that also means mentally unpacking what just happened between us. And that's something I don't have the capacity for at this point.

I start to stir next to him, and we quickly glance at one another. "It's getting late. I should probably—"

"No, yeah, of course," he stammers, standing to pull me

up with him. We gather the pizza box and beer in silence. The escape from the chaos of my life is officially over.

Rowan jumps out first, turning back to extend his arms and lifts me out. I settle inches in front of him, chest to chest. I close my eyes one last time as his hands hold the sides of my head and he kisses my forehead gingerly. I breathe him in.

"Let's go home."

The drive is short, but I use the remaining time to fill Rowan in about my mom. He's earned the truth. He absorbed the story slowly, and I sense empathy spilling from his glances. I tell him because I need to tell someone. Someone who knows how it feels to be abandoned. Rowan's quiet while I talk but offers me his hand, and before I know it, I'm sitting in Lola's driveway, staring at the empty front steps at Gramps. Déjà vu, just like this day started. Rowan's thumb rubs gently on my leg, pulling me out of my anxious cycle.

"You can do this, Scarlett," he says, his voice full of conviction.

He thinks too highly of me because I'm not so sure I can.

"And what if I can't? I don't know what to say to him, Rowan. He lied to me for nineteen years." I bite my bottom lip to keep it from quivering.

Rowan inhales deeply, his eyes tracing the floor of the truck. "Sometimes we lie to the people we love to protect them."

I know what he is saying is true. I've lied to Gramps because I knew the truth would hurt him, disappoint him. I was protecting him from who I was.

"Thanks." I sniffle and offer a small smile. This isn't how I wanted our evening to end.

Rowan nods willfully at me, and I steal one more glimpse of him, still in disbelief that he likes *me* after all this.

We get out and start to walk our separate ways, both off to fight our own unspoken battles. Before we turn in, he yells out across the yard.

"Hey, Scar!"

"Yeah?"

"I'm right here if you need me." He bows his head toward the front door, and my heart warms. Even if I did need him, I wouldn't come to him tonight. Rowan James is too good to be dragged through this storm.

The frigid air in Gramps's house is a stark contrast to the humid blanket that surrounded me in Rowan's truck. The glow of the TV illuminates Gramps in his chair with his legs kicked up, watching a fishing competition. On the side table next to him rests the envelope Mom left this morning. It's unclear if it's been opened, and I'm not sure it's my place to ask, so I move along.

"Daisy, come on, babe. It's time to eat!" My high-pitched tone masks the unease stirring inside me.

Daisy bounces off the sofa and pummels into me, nosing my hands until I scoop kibble into her ceramic bowl. At least she's unbothered by today's events.

Gramps hasn't made a peep, and I stand, stonewalled in the doorway of the kitchen as Daisy chomps noisily on her dinner behind me. I selfishly hope he's already asleep so I can shower this day off me and pretend it didn't happen. At least until tomorrow morning. Because this is tomorrow Scarlett's problem.

But then a hand reaches down to pull the lever, and Gramps sits upright in his recliner with his back to me. Neither of us speaks. It's just the low buzz of the TV and Daisy lapping water.

"Good girl," I whisper and scratch her ears, causing her tail to thump harder against the floor.

"You hungry?" Gramps asks.

I don't answer right away, but he continues anyway.

"Lola made quiche and a salad. Rowan didn't come home for dinner, so she brought the other half over for you."

My arms protectively cross my chest, and I'm filled with sudden guilt for spending the day floating in the ocean and disappearing with Rowan. I'm supposed to be here with Gramps.

The more the silence passes, the larger the elephant in the room grows—until I can't ignore it anymore. I give in and kick myself off the kitchen wall, making my way over to stand in front of Gramps's recliner.

He looks at me from the seat. His reading glasses rest on his lap, but there's no book in sight. He had to have opened the envelope. My chest fills with hot air. I want to know what she said to him. I want to know that she didn't cause him any more hurt.

"I'm sorry I wasn't here," he starts.

I pinch my eyebrows together, unsure at first what he means. Sadness covers his face, and he taps a finger on the card next to him. He crosses his legs, bringing his hands together on his lap when I don't say anything.

"You didn't know she would come here." I'm unsure why I'm defending him.

"I don't know what she said to you, Scarlett." He swallows and closes his eyes.

I want to reach forward and hold his hand, to tell him it's okay. For both of us. He looks like he might cry, but the wound inside of me keeps my feet firmly planted on the ground.

"She had no right to barge right into your life like that. She had no right to reappear out of nowhere," he says, bitterness lacing his voice.

"It wasn't out of nowhere, though, was it?" I reply. "She sent mail. Cards. Money. I mean, why didn't you cash the checks? Why didn't I get that money?"

"Scarlett, it's not that simple—" His voice grows louder as he straightens up in his chair.

"Were there *just* cards, or were there phone calls too? How could Mimi lie to me all those years too? I don't even know who you two are." My arms flail, my voice hoarse from the agonizing screeching escaping my lips. As I spiral, his face contorts with hurt. I've never yelled at Gramps, even as a little girl. I never had a reason to until now.

"Scarlett Ray, we did what we had to do." His voice is stern, and his blue eyes morph into a darker shade like the ocean before a storm.

"How could you? Did you even love Mom? She wanted to be part of my life." My voice cracks as I freely speak, lashing every thought into words. There's a burning in my eyes, but no wetness comes to their aid. Maybe there is a limit to how much you can feel in one day.

His mouth opens, but I'm met with silence.

I look at the green recliner Gramps is resting in. It's been in our living room for as long as I can remember. He'd rock me in it when I was undeniably too big to be rocked and read me my favorite mystery books. There are countless photos of him and me in the chair together, both of us always wearing a grin. It was my safety. He was my rock. He was the father my mother never gave me, the grandpa every little girl deserves, the teacher I'd be forever grateful to have, my friend when I had none. Now I look at him, and a sense of loss settles into my heart. Nothing about this makes sense.

It's too much. The air in the room is unbearable, crushing against my chest. A large breath leaves my lungs with force.

"I'm going to shower," I finally snap. I call for Daisy to follow me and leave Gramps sitting alone.

I keep squeezing more vanilla salt scrub onto my hands, rubbing until my arms are red, whisking away the memories of where Rowan's lips softly grazed my body. I scrub my skin until I can't feel my mother's words crawling across it. The water is scalding, but the pricking of my skin helps remind me I'm not numb.

I nearly trip over Daisy when I step out of the shower and grab the wall in frustration. She must've pushed the door open and curled up at the tub, waiting for me. She always finds me when I'm upset. But this time, I took so long that she fell asleep. I bend down to kiss her black nose.

"I'm sorry, girl. Don't worry about me. Everything will be okay," I coo, unsure who I'm really reassuring—me or her. She lets out a tiny sigh, and I continue to dry myself off.

It's only seven o'clock, far too early to turn in, but I sit on my bed after the shower anyway. From here, I see the side of Lola's house.

Maybe if I had a normal life, maybe if I had my shit together, maybe if I wasn't like *this*, then it could work. But there isn't a way I can see, in this world, where Rowan James and Scarlett Ray Peterson can be together. It's a tempting dream that will linger on my heart. This evening was memorable, but it was just a fluke. I know that. It's only a matter of time before he realizes too.

Two rapt knocks sound on the bedroom door, pulling me from the self-loathing thoughts. I glance at Daisy, then down at my tie-dye shirt. There's nothing left to defend.

"Come in," I mumble.

Gramps pushes the door open slowly, his face tired. A shoebox-sized container rests under his right arm. It looks old and has a flowery design on it. Not dissimilar to all the other boxes Mimi used to keep in her closet. I wonder how many times my eyes grazed over this very box without realizing the secrets it held.

"These are yours." He walks across the room and sets it on the nightstand as I spool my wet hair around my fingers. I want to stop acting like a moody teenager holed up in her bedroom, but my mind has me paralyzed.

Gramps pulls the door shut behind him. It takes a few minutes for me to build up the courage to grab the box. It's light in my hands, which is cruelly ironic. Resting my palms on the floral top, my eyes trace the lines of the ceiling.

"It's now or never, Daisy," I say as Daisy inches closer to me on the bed.

The top of the old container lifts off with ease and reveals nineteen envelopes in various sizes and colors.

KATHERINE BITNER

Nineteen birthdays of unheard wishes.

Chapter Thirteen

I t's not until Daisy drops her body down on the side of the road in the sandy grass that I pull my phone out of my pocket to check the time. It's almost noon. We've been walking for an hour now. Shading my eyes, I spin around to look at the billowy clouds behind me. The sky's growing dark, which can only mean a summer storm is in the forecast, and by the looks of it, if I don't turn around now, Daisy and I will be trapped in it. I'm not sure she'll forgive me if she gets rained on.

"Come on, Daisy. Up," I command, tugging her leash. She rolls her eyes.

"I'm sorry. We have to get home. You don't want to get stuck in this, do you?" Raising my arms toward the sky, I plead with her again, pulling on the leash as she reluctantly rolls onto her paws, grunting. I can't blame her. We've walked further than she's used to. I had to keep moving just to keep my ceaseless thoughts from rooting any deeper. It's probably been more than four miles.

We start trudging back in the unbearably humid heat, and the roads are quiet. It's Tuesday, and the only silver lining is Lu might have an answer about my van. My phone is sticky against my sweaty face, but I call Lu anyway, needing to fill the silence.

"Coastal Motor Garage, this is Lu," he greets over a loud clanking in the background.

"Hey, Lu. This is Scarlett. I dropped off the Volkswagen van . . ." I stop talking when he starts making grunting noises. I'm about to ask him if I should call another time, but Lu lets out a sigh.

"Yes, ma'am. We're working on it right now."

Something that sounds like a saw rings out in the background. Visions of them chopping my baby up momentarily cloud my mind.

"Oh! Okay, so what's wrong exactly?" I quicken my pace after looking up and seeing dark clouds roll in. I patiently wait for Lu to answer my question, but he's busy chatting with someone else. It's so noisy in the garage, I pull the phone away from my face to save my ears.

"Ha! There's a few things. Along with the battery, you needed two new spark plugs, an alignment, your tires are bald as a bowling ball, and an oil change. You had almost no oil, you know that?" He gruffly laughs, and my nose crinkles in response. Gramps told me to change the oil, but I thought that was more of a *suggestion*.

"We needed to order a part . . . so you'll have to wait 'til Thursday, all right? You can pick it up then around five."

"Thanks, Lu. I'll see ya Thursday," I reply kindly.

A pit forms in my stomach as I hang up. Though I can't pretend to know what half that stuff means, I know it can't be a cheap repair. Gramps is friends with Lu and swears up and down he is an honest man who won't upcharge me a cent. But it still stings.

Those birthday checks would come in handy right about now.

Thunder claps loudly overhead as I drag Daisy into the house. I notice Gramps on the screened-in back porch, the white rocker gently moving. I apologize to Daisy for the hundredth time for making her walk so far and fill her bowl with water. She'll probably sleep until tomorrow, but a little exercise is good for her.

"It builds character," I remind her.

Standing in the dimly lit kitchen, I mindlessly pour iced tea into a tall glass, and Gramps clears his throat on the porch. The sliding door is cracked open, making the screen the only thing between us. Our last interaction was when he set the cards on the nightstand yesterday. This morning, he drove to the post office, and by the looks of the box on the kitchen counter, Lola brought him breakfast. My stomach grumbles. Four miles of walking worked up my appetite.

I peer out the kitchen window. Rowan's truck is still missing from the driveway. It's been gone since I woke up at eight. We haven't spoken since parting ways, and I let that fact linger a moment too long, long enough for me to realize I might actually *miss* his company. I have the urge to text him about my walk all the way to the pier. Maybe when I see him later I can ask him to drive me to Lu's on Thursday. That seems like a practical excuse to steal a little more time with him.

I watch the edge of the rocker roll gently back and forth and take a steadying breath, running my hand up and down the glass, letting the condensation calm me. I need to go talk to him.

"Scarlett." Gramps looks up at me as I silently pad onto the porch. I settle in the chair across from him. Thunder rolls in the distance, an appropriate backdrop to the conversation I assume we are about to have.

"Did you open the cards?" he asks.

He could've just looked in my room and seen the box unmoved, but Gramps would never invade my privacy like that. I lift my tired head and shake it *no*. No more running from this.

Gramps nods and runs his palms along the armrests of the rocker. "There's a lot to this story, Scar. I think it's time you know. All of it."

"I'm ready," I reassure him, rubbing my hands nervously against my thighs. I'm not ready, but the truth doesn't wait for a good time.

His mind appears to stray beyond us for a moment before he pulls himself back to me. "First, I want you to know that Mimi knew everything." He points a finger at me, but his voice is gentle.

I nod and mouth a mousey, "Okay."

"When your mom first ran away, we didn't hear from her for a whole year. She told us she needed to clear her head, and as worried as we were about her, we were glad she didn't take you with her. We worried about *you* most. It took you a whole year to readjust after she left. But you did it, you remember that?"

I nod. I suppressed it for so long, but in the faint light, the confusion, hurt, and sleepless nights that riddled me *year after year* come crashing into me.

Gramps clears his throat. "You had just turned eight when she called for the first time. She asked to speak with you, but we couldn't allow it. Your mother was in a bad place, strung out on drugs. We told her we'd help her, but we had to protect you. Mimi stayed with you, and I went to find her to put her in rehab. We made sure she got the best care she could get, but the rule was she couldn't see you until she was better. You were such a forgiving kid. You would've run to her and forgave her, and she would've broken your heart time and time again, Scar. I couldn't allow it."

I pinch my lips together as tight as I can, holding the tears that threaten to spill. Gramps's voice is scratchy in his throat, his hand rubbing his stubble.

"Rehab didn't last long, but we continued to send her money for years. She always had access to the best care. But you can't make someone change if they don't want to change themselves. When you were ten, she disappeared again, telling us to never come looking for her, she was done with us."

Gramps pauses, letting a breath out, but I stay silent, no longer rocking. I let him gather himself.

"She relinquished custody to us, and other than the cards to you, we didn't hear from her—until we got a letter when you were about fifteen. She told us she was two years sober and married to a doctor who had three kids of his own. She said she was happy."

Gramps pinches his mouth into a line and looks at me, shrugging slightly. The shrug says everything. He couldn't save her. After all this time, she broke his heart, along with mine. All this time, I never knew how much he gave of himself to try to save her, to protect me. Why

125

did I never realize that she abandoned him too?

"The reason we never gave you those birthday cards was because they would've just hurt you more. I know it's painful to think she chose another life. We knew she'd never come back, and we couldn't see the hope in your eyes burn out every year. She chose another life, but we would always choose *you*. Again and again, Scarlett Ray, we'd choose you." His mouth curls into a sorrowful smile, a beg for forgiveness.

I open my mouth, but my head simply hangs, shaking back and forth. The strength of the tears break my efforts to hold them back, and they quietly pour onto my cheeks. Gramps lets me have the moment.

"I had no idea," I manage to say, searching my head for the next right thing to say. How do you tell someone you love them, you forgive them, you're sorry for how you reacted, you're sorry for how they had to protect you, and you're sorry that someone else broke their heart?

"I'm sorry you found out this way. I never wanted to tell you, and your mom coming here was my worst nightmare. But you're not a little girl anymore, Scar."

"Did you read the letter she left you?"

He nods. "I did. I always read what she writes. She told me she is sorry for missing Mimi's funeral and that she wants to pay me back for all those years of rehab."

I shake my head, concealing a sharp laugh. Nothing about this is funny. She missed her own mother's funeral. Though, I'm not sure I'd go to hers.

"I didn't read her cards or open the envelope she left me," I admit to Gramps, wishing he would tell me what the right choice is, but he won't. He never does. He never pushes me in one way or another.

"You'll do what you need to do." He nods at me.

We sit in silence a little longer, until he coaxes me out of my rocking chair to pull me into a hug.

"I love you," he murmurs, holding me tightly to him.

I bury my face in his shoulder and breath in the coffee and peppermint smell laden on his shirt. I wipe my eyes as I pull away and whisper back, "I love you too, Gramps. Always."

He squeezes my shoulders. "Movie night?" he asks, and I nod, smiling behind the tears. I tell him I'll meet him in the living room in a little bit. There's something I need to do first.

I march into the guest room. The unopened box glares at me from the bed. It's beckoning me to open it, to indulge the cards it contains. There is only one thing I wanted to do with the cards. Because there is only one person in this world who still means something to me, and that person never left. In fact, he is waiting for me in the other room.

Popping the top off, I stare at the pile of nineteen cards. My name is scribbled across each envelope, but it doesn't feel like they belong to me. Leaning over the side of the bed, I grab the trash can and, in one fell swoop, dump the contents of the box into the trash can. They fall in with a thud, and I let out a breath that felt like it had been trapped inside for years.

I grab the thick manila envelope, the one my mother set on the table for me. With trembling hands, I search for the strength to rip it open. I know what is inside has the ability to hurt me, but I can't hide from it any longer. With eyes squeezed shut, I tear it open, and the weight of the contents falls onto my lap in a single lump.

I open one eye cautiously, then open both wide as a stack of cash stares back at me. A single rubber band wraps around a thick stack of hundred-dollar bills with a sticky note stuck to it. Scribbled in pen on the tiny piece of paper are two simple words: *I'm sorry.*

I trace the indentation of her writing with my finger. Cursive and messy. I look with continued disbelief that I'm looking at my mom's handwriting. The woman who dropped me off at summer camp and never came back. The mom I thought was gone—forever. The mom I never bothered to look for because I had Mimi and Gramps. The mom who has the same blonde hair as me and taught me how to swim in the ocean.

But that's not who left me more cash than I've made in the last year. The person who left me this is someone who is riddled with guilt, someone who thinks she can simply buy forgiveness.

Gramps snores in his recliner, his head lolled to the side, as the end credits roll on his big-screen TV. Stretching, I quietly beckon Daisy toward the front door to let her out one more time before we turn in for the night.

Rowan's truck lights break through the darkness, triggering the floodlights surrounding Lola's property. I cross my arms over my chest, self-conscious in the oversized T-shirt I wear to bed, and walk toward the truck. It seems stupid, considering Rowan saw me completely unclothed the night before.

My cheeks flush as Rowan steps out of the truck. Daisy beats me to him though, barreling by to greet Rowan. He kneels, scratching her neck.

"Hey," I say shyly, tiptoeing through the grass toward

him. His normal glow is replaced by a look of fatigue, complete with under-eye bags and dirty clothes. To my knowledge, Rowan doesn't have a job. Or maybe I don't know him enough to know the small details of his life. No matter how much I wish I did.

It's too late, Scar. You're leaving in four days.

"Hey." His voice echoes his appearance. He doesn't look up but continues to scratch Daisy's ears. I glare with jealousy for a moment as she gives me the side-eye. There's no doubt Daisy would leave me for Rowan.

"Long day?" I muster up a smile, but Rowan still avoids eye contact, running a hand over his messy hair and raising his eyebrows.

"Long, but good." His eyes finally meet mine, and there's a look I don't recognize. About to open my mouth, he juts his thumb over his shoulder toward the house. "I'm so sorry, Scarlett. I'd love to talk, but I'm downright exhausted." He leans forward and plants a quick kiss on my forehead.

"Right, of course. G' night," I utter as I force a smile and grab Daisy by the collar so she follows me, and not Rowan, home.

Before turning off my lamp, I gaze out the window. Rowan's light is off. A deep sigh escapes my chest as I pull Daisy closer so that she's huddled next to me. She smells like mud and kibble, but I don't care. I need someone to hold tonight.

I fall asleep thinking about running into the Pacific Ocean.

Chapter Fourteen

The envelope full of cash is the first thing I see when I wake up. Well, that and Daisy's face. I shove her gently to the side, and she grumbles like an old lady. The stack of cash stares at me daringly, but I don't have an answer for it yet. It feels like dirty money. I'm not as confident in myself as Gramps is in me, and I've never expected to be in a situation as layered as this. Add Rowan's standoffishness and my ability to overthink everything to the mix, and you've got the perfect storm.

Dark-roast coffee waits in the pot for me by the time I mosey to the kitchen. I quietly grab a mug from the cabinet and pour myself a steaming cup while Gramps sits at the kitchen table, the newspaper open in front of him. I always thought it strange that Gramps was a firm believer in news being read and not watched. But now I kind of understand the appeal of slowing down.

We exchange "good mornings" as I lean against the counter, my tie-dye pajamas a colorful contrast to the white kitchen. Gramps eyes don't stray from the paper, and I search my groggy brain for the right way to phrase my question. But I can't find it, so I blurt out the jumbled thoughts in my head.

"I opened it, Gramps. I opened the envelope from Mom," I break the silence, clutching the hot coffee cup to my chest.

Gramps's head stays down, but his eyes peer over the top of his glasses, so I continue to ramble.

"So . . . she left me with cash. Like *a lot* of cash. More cash than I've ever seen in person. I don't understand why she would do that." As I say it, a weight drifts off my shoulders.

Gramps releases the paper, and he pulls off his glasses, twirling them in one hand. "Huh. Probably did that so you couldn't give it back, considering we never cashed her checks." He sips his coffee, flipping the newspaper to the other side.

"Yeah, maybe. But she also scribbled a note that said, *I'm sorry.*' I mean, why now?" I throw my hands up, nearly spilling my coffee. "I know you think I can figure this all out on my own, or at least at my age you believe I should be able to . . . But Gramps, I honestly don't know what the hell to do." My breathy speech finally makes him pause and give me his full attention.

"Take it from me, don't waste time trying to figure out *why* she does anything. Forget about that." He places the paper down. "What do you want to do?" he asks, holding up a finger objectively as I start to open my mouth. "Not what you think *I* want you to do or what *she* thinks you'll do. What do *you* want to do, Scarlett?"

I'm back to being sixteen in the kitchen with Mimi and Gramps, listening to their speeches on growing up.

I don't hesitate this time, though.

"I want to use it for my trip. Is that wrong of me?"

Gramps claps loudly once. "There's your answer! She gave it to you for a reason, Scar. Probably guilt, but hey, that doesn't mean *you* need to feel guilty for using it. You've been working so hard for this trip, and now you can do it with a safety net. She gave you a *gift*. And it's the only one she's ever given you."

There are so many things I can do with this "gift." It's more than enough for the trip. It may even be enough to settle somewhere—eventually.

However, Gramps is wrong about something. It's not the only gift she's ever given me. She gave me a life with him.

With only a few days left in the Outer Banks, I want to make sure I spend as much time with Gramps as I can. Rowan's truck was gone when I woke up, and I haven't seen him running or at the beach. So when Gramps suggests we get lunch in town, I happily oblige, thankful for the distraction.

At the diner, the waitress drops off lunch at our table: a Reuben for me and an Italian sub for Gramps. We sit in the same booth he always sits in at the diner, and it's comforting to me to think Gramps has a rooted life here. He has his friends, waitresses who know him by name, a favorite bench on the pier, and a booth at the diner. It gives me reassurance that I'm not leaving him here to fend for himself. If anything, I'll be the one who's alone.

I pop a chip from the paper-lined basket into my

mouth. "Lu says I can pick up the van on Thursday evening. There was a lot to fix, I guess, but he swears he'll get it all done." I smile at Gramps and take a gulp of cola.

He nods, wiping the crumbs from his mouth, and places his sub back on the plate. "Lu's a reliable guy. If he says it'll be done, it'll be done."

He steals a chip from my basket. I let him.

"Has he given you the total yet?"

"Not yet, but I'm sure he will. But now I have the money to pay for it." I feel good for once that I am taking care of something myself. Even if it's blood-money from my estranged mother paying my way.

"Nonsense. I'm paying for it," Gramps says, picking up his sub again.

"Gramps, no. You've done enough for me."

He pauses, the sub midair, his old eyes kind but meaning business. "This isn't up for discussion. I'm paying for it. Just 'cause I'm old, doesn't mean you can boss me around."

I gasp, but we both laugh. "Okay, Gramps. You know I appreciate it."

He grins with his mouth shut, full of sub, and crumbs down the front of his green, fishing T-shirt.

"I'm going to miss having Daisy around," Gramps adds wistfully. The tone catches me off guard. If it wasn't for Mimi, I don't think he'd ever have an animal in the house.

"Really?" I narrow my eyes at him.

"Really. Never thought I'd say that, but she adds energy to the house. She's got spunk."

"Mimi would've loved her. Daisy would've driven her nuts with the way she lounges right under your feet, but she would've spoiled that dog rotten." A smile takes over my face, thinking about Mimi and Daisy meeting. I got

Daisy three years after she passed, but Mimi didn't meet an animal she didn't instantly love or didn't love her back.

"You sure Daisy wants to go to California too?" His eyes twinkle as he looks at me over his sandwich. I roll mine.

"I'm sure. She'll love the open road. And I've started booking some cool glamping sites and Airbnbs along the way."

"What the hell is glamping?" Gramps makes a sour face.

I respond with a full belly laugh and take a sip of cola before explaining. "It's like camping but glamorous." I put glamorous in air quotes because I'm pretty sure my version of glamorous is different from his. "So I can sleep in my van, but they have hot showers, fire pits, Wi-Fi, and some even have little cafés." My hands are animated as I talk about it. "I found some that are owned by women, for women solo campers, so they can meet and stuff. It's pretty cool."

"Well, I'll be darned. You learn something new every day! I didn't think you were the *socializing* type." He winks.

"I am . . . *trying*. I want to meet people and have friends. I just haven't . . . found my circle yet."

Gramps nods, his mouth full. The weight of my words linger in the air between us, forcing me to think about them longer than I wanted.

"What're you worried about now?" Gramps pipes up.

I stammer over my words, eventually coming out with it because there is no use in hiding anything. We hid enough between us for years. "Nothing! It's just a weird feeling. I left Asheville, and I'm not really sure I'll ever go back. There's no one there waiting for me to come back. The people I thought were friends forgot me the instant I left, and I'm beginning to think maybe that's good because I didn't really like who I was when I was there."

Gramps looks at me with discernment. His eyes blink slowly.

"It's all becoming so real. I never thought it would actually happen," I add.

Gramps lets out a soft chuckle, and my heart jumps a beat. It wasn't the reaction I was expecting, though I'm not sure exactly what I expected.

"This has always been *your* dream, Scar," he starts, his elbows leaning on the table as he crumbles a napkin in his hand. "And just because dumb people have decided to skip out on it, doesn't mean it will be any less. Do this for you."

A little laugh escapes me. Every time a guy broke my heart, Gramps would say, "They are the dumb ones." It was oddly insulting but always made me feel a little better.

"You might be right."

Gramps couldn't be more accepting of who I am, and we couldn't be more different. He worked at the same place from the time my mom was born until he retired. He was a man of habit. The only reason he moved to the island and didn't stay in Wilmington was because Mimi wanted to. And the only reason he didn't move back to Wilmington after she passed was because he was already here. "No sense in moving," he'd say. So finding steady work, a clean and safe place to live—that was what he wanted for me. I only ever did the opposite. I thought I had hidden it so well these past few years too.

The waitress drops the check off and smiles big at Gramps, asking him if she'll see him next week. He nods and pulls a worn-out leather wallet from his shirt pocket. I start to slide from the booth, but Gramps doesn't budge, his hands clasped on the table in front of him. He pulls on his baseball cap and looks up at me.

"I see the way you are, Scar. And you're not the little girl you used to be. You're finding your way, and if Asheville doesn't fit you, keep on going. You're going to find your place. You're going to find something you love." He shakes his head ever so slightly, contemplating his next words as I sit still as could be. "And no matter what, you always have a place here with me. I know living with your old Gramps isn't *glamping*."

I swallow the lump forming in my throat as he continues.

"But the room is always yours. I'm here for you, Scarlett, in between all of it." He points at me, then him.

Pursing my lips together, I nod, teary eyed. I don't know if Gramps has gotten sappier with age or if I've become a better listener.

"When did you get so mushy, Gramps?" I tease.

He straightens up in his seat but just shrugs. "I'm like a fine wine. I get better with age, honey."

I slam my palm on the table, my eyes widening. "Gramps, you did not just quote the sign hanging in Lola's dining room!"

He throws his head back laughing, proud of himself. "They are nice signs." He finally pushes himself out of the booth.

His words roll through my mind and settle in my heart. I'll need to repeat them on days that are hard, I know that. I need to keep them safe.

I have no idea where I'm going, but I'm not going back. Somewhere along the way this week, that chapter has been closed. Maybe the only way to move forward is to embrace the mess in between.

We spend the rest of the day together, running errands. It's like the old times, and I relish in it. It's been years since I drove around all afternoon with Gramps. But I push that sadness away. I'm here now with him, and I have to let that be enough. At the hardware store, Gramps introduces me to the owner, Paul. He pushes me forward to shake his hand like I'm a child, but Gramps's voice is full of pride when he tells Paul I'm his granddaughter. He tells him about my glamping trip. The two old men have a field day teasing me about it. Paul is a Vietnam veteran and proceeds to elaborate on how camping was done in *his* day. Gramps just laughs, slapping Paul on the back and beaming at me.

My chest feels tight, along with my throat as we leave the hardware store. For the last seven years, I hid, worried Gramps would find disappointment in the life I was leading. I got it wrong. Gramps has always loved exactly who I am. He's seen me for me. And it took years for me to have the courage to accept that love.

I say nothing as we hop into his old Ford truck and he clicks on the radio. Neil Diamond starts to play through the stereo, and Gramps hums along. I train my eyes to look out the window, watching the tall grass flow by on the highway. I'm going to miss this. I have to do this—for me—but it doesn't sting any less.

I'm grateful when Gramps's phone rings. He has a quick conversation, and when it's over, he smiles at me.

"Lola invited us over for dinner. Five sharp. She's making grilled salmon."

"Oh, how sweet. I'm free," I reply, my voice tight from holding back the tears that have been bubbling up through the duration of the car ride. It doesn't escape me how only a week ago I would've loathed going to Lola's. Lola and Rowan have somehow wiggled their way into my heart in the span of two weeks.

I had successfully kept thoughts about Rowan at bay today. But I don't try to suppress the smile budding on my face when I think about getting to see him tonight.

Chapter Fifteen

The distance between Lola's and Gramps's front doors is maybe fifty yards, yet somehow I manage to still run late for dinner.

"Do not look at me like that," I grumble at Daisy. Her head rests on her paws, and her brown eyes trace my scrambling movements while I attempt to find an outfit for dinner. I've tried on every combination of clothing I have, and nothing feels right. It doesn't escape me that I haven't cared this much about what I wear since my first date . . . three boyfriends ago.

"Scarlett, I'm leaving. Meet me over there!" Gramps calls out.

A small bout of panic rises in my chest. *Okay, okay, I'll just keep this one. It's fine.* I smooth my hands over the black sundress I chose. It'll have to do.

I carefully push Lola's front door open after no one responds to my knocking. Aromas of seafood waft toward me the moment I step into the colorful foyer. I wander through the living room to the kitchen, where Gramps's deep laughter and the sound of sizzling meets my ears. If I didn't know better, I'd think I'm invading a private moment with the way Gramps is leaning on Lola's island with a glass in one hand and his other gesturing about something he finds amusing. They only have eyes for each other as classical music plays from the speakers mounted around the home. The newest home improvement Rowan's been working on this week for Lola.

"She made it!" Lola exclaims.

I warily enter the kitchen. An overflowing margarita is in Lola's one hand, a kitchen towel in the other. Her hair's teased high on her head, and a smile is plastered on her bright pink lips. I grin back, slyly stealing glances around the kitchen. There's no indication that a thirty-year-old man resides here.

"The salmon will be off the grill in about five minutes, but have yourself a drink while we wait!" She shoves a palm-tree-painted margarita glass at me, and I look at Gramps with wide eyes. Lola's theatrics still stir me.

"Is Rowan here?" I keep my voice casual as I pour a healthy serving of strawberry margarita.

Lola wipes the sparkling stone countertop and shakes her head. "No. No, he isn't. He was so disappointed he couldn't make it to your last dinner, but he had plans." Lola avoids looking at me.

"Oh!" I attempt to hide the surprise in my voice. "Last dinner" sounds final and depressing, but it's not a lie, which only makes Rowan's absence even more unsettling.

"Well, I'm sure he had a good reason for missing this delicious feast." Gramps offers me a small smile.

"He had plans with someone or something, and Rowan is a man of his word," Lola adds, leaning over to open the oven. Rowan's not mentioned again as Lola pulls out roasted potatoes, setting the pan on the stovetop. I bite my lip, and Lola looks at me, her mouth falling open. "Oh, no. Oh gosh, you do eat salmon and potatoes, honey, right?"

I take a shaky breath and readjust my posture, shaking off an army of negative thoughts. "Of course. Salmon is great." I give a rigid smile. "I appreciate the dinner a lot, Lola. Thanks for having us."

"Of course, of course! We're all gonna miss you. I know it's only been a few weeks, but you've been great company." Lola tilts her head and grins at me. She'd probably pinch my cheek if I let her.

Bringing my lips to the glass edge, I sip the drink. Here's to hoping the numbing effects of the drink kick in sooner rather than later. Because while the sentiment is sweet, I'm finding it hard to believe at the moment. Not *everyone* will miss me. If that was true, *everyone* would be here. While Gramps and Lola chat, I try not to assume the worst about Lola's explanation. But I don't know how "prior plans" on a Wednesday evening could mean anything but a date.

Before Lola serves dinner, I excuse myself to the bathroom and pull my phone from my purse. Leaning against the wall, a glimpse of myself in the mirror makes me stare too long, and I look away. It was foolish to waste all that time on my outfit tonight. My mouth twists in frustration as I swipe my phone open, needing to hear from Rowan myself why he isn't here.

As my fingers hover over the keys, an incoming message from Rowan lights up my screen.

Rowan: I'm so sorry I had to miss dinner tonight. A last minute thing came up and I had to take care of it.

141

I can still drive you to your car tomorrow! Pick you up at 5?

A hiccup of laughter leaves my throat, and I tilt my head to the ceiling. I should've never gotten attached. I knew better.

I forcefully hold the power button, shutting down my phone completely. End of conversation.

I *am* leaving tomorrow and don't have the energy to hold onto hope in the eleventh hour over Rowan. No matter how desperately I longed to kiss him tonight after dinner.

My phone slides back into my purse, and I take a deep breath, composing myself before joining Lola and Gramps at the dining table. I didn't come to the Outer Banks for Rowan anyway. He was simply an unplanned detour.

Dinner's delicious, which is no surprise to me. I'll miss Lola's home-cooked meals she's constantly bringing out. Thankfully, even as I sit there quietly, Gramps and Lola keep the conversation flowing.

One thing is certain, the chemistry between Lola and Gramps is unquestionable. It's entirely different from him and Mimi. Gramps loved Mimi dearly, and he would've done anything for her. They had a love that was classic, and though they always took care of each other, it wasn't until this trip that I realized their life wasn't easy like I'd always imagined it had been. They lost a child who still lived and became parents to a young child as they were nearing fifty, all while working to stay afloat and shield me from the cruel realities of my mother. When I graduated high school and left, Gramps sold his business in Wilmington and moved to the Outer Banks to give Mimi the life of retirement she dreamed of. So when she died, my heart broke twice. Once because I was losing a mother and grandmother all in one, but then a second time for Gramps and the future he wouldn't get to experience with her.

But now as I sit here at the dining table, seeing the unexpected companionship flow between him and Lola, the last bit of hesitation over leaving evaporates. I'm not the only thing holding Gramps's life together. He's stronger than I ever realized. And Lola is a good person. She's the friend he needs, the company I know he desired, even if he is too stubborn to have ever admitted it to me.

Glancing right, the empty dining chair mocks me. I hope one day I'll get to experience a fraction of the love Gramps has. Every time I think I'm coming close to it, it dissolves into thin air, leaving me wondering if it ever existed at all.

"Are you sure you have to go?" Lola makes a pouty face over the dinner table.

"Yes, it's time, I think," I reply, pulling myself from my fog. I meet Gramps's loving gaze.

"Well, when you are finished adventuring, you must come back to visit. It's nice to have some youthfulness around here. You and Rowan keep us young!" She laughs, elbowing Gramps.

He chuckles, bowing his head in agreement.

"I'll be back. I promise." I pointedly look at Gramps as I say it. Because I do promise to come back.

I just hope Rowan is long gone when I do.

Once we're done eating the three-course meal and saying our goodbyes, Gramps and I walk back, arm in arm, with one hand on our bellies, full as can be. The summer sky is dark, and I stub my toe on the driftwood piece that Daisy has dragged halfway up the front porch steps.

"Dammit!" I hop up and down, grabbing my foot. I bend down and shove the wood back into the yard before Gramps trips too.

"She's going to miss that. That was a solid piece of wood. She beelines for it every morning," he replies, totally ignoring me limping on one foot. I curse a few more times under my breath.

"She'll get over it. There's plenty of wood in this world. I'll find her a better stick on our journey," I reply curtly.

"Good luck convincing her of that. She's a smart cookie." He winks and turns around, pushing open the front door.

I stand there for another beat, my foot still throbbing. Something in his conviction tells me he isn't talking about the piece of dried-up wood on his front lawn. My eyes wander over to the empty spot in the driveway where the black truck should be parked.

She has no other choice but to get over it. The damn piece of wood is staying *here.*

Chapter Sixteen

I wake up with a weird feeling in my body. A tightness in my chest is matched by the rippling wave of anxiety rolling through my body. It's my last day here before I drive west. I keep calling it my adventure because calling it six-to-nine weeks of unknown driving sounds less appealing, and if I keep thinking of it like that, I'll freak myself out of going.

I stayed up late last night, later than I should've, finalizing my plans. It's the most organized I've ever been in my life, and along with the past whirlwind two weeks I've had, I feel even more out of it. In my head, I know that, logically, I should be feeling better about things coming together, but my heart is full of flitty little butterflies.

In the past, when I've planned this drive, it was always a slightly different route with every different partner. I've never gotten around to planning the nitty-gritty details, though. Not until now. I should be happy about it.

A static radio station plays in the kitchen as I routinely walk into the room. The radio hosts announce the temperature of the day—another hot and humid scorcher. As if it would be anything else.

Splayed out like a beached seal, Daisy has taken up residence under Gramps's legs at the kitchen table, her tan snout resting on top of his loafers. I bite my tongue before I repeat how she'll miss him. I refuse to let myself be sad today. Today will be a good day.

"Coffee is made, eggs are in the pan, and Lola dropped some cinnamon rolls off," Gramps rattles off from behind the newspaper propped up on the table.

I smirk to myself, eyeing up the huge casserole dish of homemade cinnamon rolls.

"What's the plan today?" Folding his paper down over the empty breakfast plate, Gramps studies me over his reading glasses. The smell of sweet cinnamon rolls jolts me awake with a burst of sugar, and I take a gulp of coffee before answering him.

"Well, I'm pretty much packed. I just wish I could get my van back earlier. Do you think if we stop over there earlier today, Lu might have it ready?" I ask, eager for the first time in my life to be early for anything.

Gramps clicks his tongue and wags his head. "Lu's on island time, m' dear. If he said five o'clock, he means he will be *starting* the last touch at five. Don't worry. It will be ready before you leave."

I pinch my lips together in response. Five it is.

"Okay . . . then there isn't much I need to do actually. I

mean, I'd love to go down to the beach with Daisy. Maybe we can get lunch at the diner? Oh, and I need to stop at the Piggly Wiggly to get some snacks. For the road tomorrow." As I speak, my body becomes riddled with unexpected emotions. Goodbyes are coming, and Gramps and I aren't good at goodbyes. We never have been.

"Scarlett Ray Peterson," Gramps says, making me snap out of my head. He doesn't wait for me to respond before pulling off his readers and leaning in toward me over the kitchen table. "Chin up. There is no reason in the world to feel sad today. If Mimi was here, she'd be shaking your shoulders and making you ham sandwiches for the road." His finger points at me, but the corners of his mouth curl up, as does mine in response.

I roll my eyes. He is right. I've got to shake this.

"Now, *I'm* not going to make you sandwiches for the road, but there will be no tears at my breakfast table. Don't waste this opportunity. You're meant to go."

I stare at him over my coffee mug. Gramps is either a man of no words or it's a lofty speech, rallying me up.

"Gramps, what if I step foot in California and I decide it's home?" I bite my lip, nervous for his answer.

"Then you better send me a friggin' postcard," he replies clear as day.

I laugh, taken aback by his lightness. It's so different than it was seven years ago when I left for college. He let me go, but not without struggle. It took me years to realize he might've been worried I'd wind up like his own daughter, leaving him and Mimi in the dark. But I wasn't my mother. I'd always come back, even if it wasn't permanently.

I had one more question for him.

"How did *you* know where home was?"

Gramps looks at me, then past me. "Home was never a place for me, Scar. It was a person."

My breath catches in my throat. "I hope I find that someday. What you two had," I admit, looking at the coffee in my mug.

"You will. But don't forget, home is here too." He puts his hand briefly over his chest. "Make a home in your own heart, and you'll never feel lost."

"Okay . . . is that on Lola's wall?" I joke, breaking the heaviness of this conversation, even though every word is hitting me in the core.

Gramps cackles, slapping his knee and shaking his head slowly. "No, that's all me, baby. Gramps's words of wisdom!" He flashes a bright smile that reaches his eyes.

Gramps and I spent the afternoon together. We took Daisy to the beach, where she chased seagulls and rolled in the wet sand until every inch of her was covered in damp muck. At lunch, we sat in our usual booth in the diner, again, and Gramps insisted I tell him my routed plan—for the third time. We make a pact to talk every day, so he knows where I am and where I'm heading next. The more I talk about the trip, the more the excitement and nerves grow in my chest.

After lunch, Gramps goes home to take a nap, and I drive his truck to the Piggly Wiggly, prepped with a long, mental list of road fuel—aka a list of snacks to keep me going for my long drives ahead. I've made the decision to put as much distance between me and the coast of North Carolina as I can the first day. *Rip the bandage off.*

Strolling down the fluorescently lit aisles, I mindlessly grab for food without thought, tossing item after item in my basket. I don't even mind it, being alone in this. Well, until I stop at something I want on the top shelf and curse my vertically challenged body. There's no one in the aisle with me, so I teeter on my tiptoes, pulling myself up on the metal shelves, when a long arm reaches over my shoulder from out of nowhere, grabbing what I have my eyes so intensely focused on.

In the blink of an eye, I go from murmuring "thanks" to speechlessly staring into those seductive hazel eyes. I release my grip on the shelf, letting out a small huff when my heels slam onto the floor. *Calm down, body. We are trying not to care about him anymore.*

He doesn't say a word as he holds out the bag of chips toward me. My eyes stay on his hand, avoiding his eyes, and I gently take the chips from him, balancing them on my wildly overflowing shopping basket. I ignore how the metal handles dig into my arm with the weight and mumble, "Thanks," before turning my attention back to the shelf.

In a quick glance, I clock the bottle of rosé in his hands. Lola hates wine, and Rowan only likes beer. *So he says.* There's a gnawing at my gut. I'm leaving, and he probably has a hot date set up for this weekend. My chest suddenly feels tight, and the temptation to drop my basket and leave the store is strong. For a split second, I try to convince myself I'll survive without road-trip snacks.

"You know, they make carts so you don't have to break your back." His tone is joking, but his face is searching.

"I like the challenge," I reply dryly.

He lets out a small laugh but doesn't look at me anymore.

"Lola said dinner was really nice last night—" he starts, but I readjust the basket on my other arm, interrupting him quickly.

"It was. You really missed out on a good one!" Abruptly, I start walking toward the checkout. I can't handle this goodbye. Not when it feels like I just said hello.

"I should've been there. That wasn't cool of me to miss the dinner, Scar. I'm sorry. Can I see you tonight?" he calls out, jogging to catch up with me. His smell wafts toward me, and I wish it didn't do what it does to me.

I abruptly swivel, again, to face him. Rowan's shoulders slump forward a bit, and he closes in on me. His face is tense, maybe even anxious. *Good.*

"I am leaving, Rowan. Tomorrow at 7:00 a.m. sharp. I don't have time for this."

His head drops a bit, and I sense a few prying eyes watching us. With fists clenched, Rowan purses his lips tightly before expelling a slow breath.

"I deserve that. If you need any help getting packed, or anything at all, just let me know. Okay?" He stumbles over his words, and I nod, unsure how to respond. He turns around to walk back into the aisle we came from. As I place my stuff on the belt, the cashier eyes me curiously, but I pull out my phone, pretending to be doing something. I'm in no mood for small talk.

When I glance over my shoulder, Rowan's long gone.

Chapter Seventeen

At five on the dot, Gramps drops me off in the parking lot of Lu's Garage. He tells me he'll meet me at home and peels out of the gravel parking before I can even ask about payment. Maybe he forgot he told me he'd pay. Dropping my hands to my side, I pace into the garage anyway. My van's not sitting out front like it should be.

Lu twists in his old desk chair, wearing the same blue grease-stained jumper as before. He looks up under his white, bushy eyebrows.

"Miss Scarlett," he says fondly.

"Hi, Lu. I, uh, I don't see my van out front?" I swing around to look out front again, hoping I just missed it. Though, that seems nearly impossible. Lu isn't fazed as he haphazardly shifts papers around on his desk until a crinkled slip of yellow transfer paper appears.

"Here is all the work we did on it. She'll run like a Cadillac now! Fresh oil and tires, a bunch of other stuff I already tol' Ray 'bout. Put AC in that death trap too. So you're good to go."

The paper he hands me is just a sheet full of smeared chicken-scratch writing, so I patiently wait for an invoice.

"Oh, um, it's out back. The keys are in the front seat," he says enthusiastically, but I don't move.

"Okay, but what do I owe you?"

"You owe nothing. A little birdy already paid the bill." Lu winks at me, pulling the dangling toothpick from his mouth.

Very slick, Gramps.

Lu then points over his shoulder to the exit door. "Van's back there, honey."

Grinning, I fold the paper into my pocket and thank Lu, doing an awkward skip-run out the exit into the back of the garage.

The white top of the van grabs my eye out by the second workshop. Gramps mentioned to me on our drive over that Lu rents the workshop out to a carpenter or something like that. I let out a sigh of relief and pick up my pace, anxious to get my baby back. But my pace halts when Rowan steps from the workshop and waves, walking toward me.

"Rowan, what are you doing here?" My feet stop a few feet in front of him, and I let my eyes trail him up and down. Rowan doesn't have the same outfit on as he did in the grocery store. He's dressed nicely in a short-sleeved button-down and khaki shorts. He looks good, though he's never looked bad. My long, bohemian skirt drags along the pine needles when I take two more steps toward him.

"Before you get in your van, I need to say some things to you," he starts, his hands coming together to crack his knuckles in front of his chest.

"Whatever you have to say . . . it doesn't matter."

"I know you're leaving, Scar." He uses the nickname I've only allowed him and Gramps to ever use. I wonder if he knows that.

Rowan James has an undeniable silent magic with the way he causes my thoughts to spill out of me. "Listen, I've been thinking," I inhale slowly, fiddling with my skirt while he watches me, his eyes slightly narrowed. "Maybe I made *this* into something it isn't." I point between us. "It certainly wouldn't be the first time I've done that. You're just a friend, and that's fine, because maybe that is all it was ever meant to be. And honestly, it's probably for the best because I'm not staying."

His eyebrows go up, but he's not frowning. I ignore it and continue, unable to stop my train of thought.

"I'm going to be gone for weeks, maybe months. I don't really have a plan. I just know it's time to go. There's some stuff I have to figure out—for me. And I really enjoyed . . . *everything* . . . and if things were different, then—"

He steps forward, abruptly cutting off my rambling. Rowan's hands gently cup the sides of my face, and his chest presses against me as his lips hover near mine. "Hold your thought, Scar," he says, and my mind quiets instantly, our breath the only audible sound between us. Leaning forward in synchrony, the space between our lips disappears, and my eyes shut, allowing Rowan to kiss me so tenderly it takes my breath away. When he pulls away, the heat lingers between us, our eyes locked on each other.

"Why did you do that?" I whisper. One kiss and every wall I've built up this week wavers, threatening to fall over with one more touch.

"Because it's all I've been thinking about for the past three days. You have no idea how badly I've wanted to see you, to hold you again."

"What?" I cry out. "You've literally avoided me for the last three days. Are you delusional, or am I?"

He starts laughing, making me step back, miffed. I tightly cross my arms, unsure if I want to kiss him again or slap him.

"Why are you laughing? Stop!" I hiss, but he continues to chuckle. Then his smile turns serious, and he places a hand on my shoulder, reluctantly spinning me around.

"Please, will you just go look at your van?" he pleads, clearly amused by my discomfort.

I shrug his hands off but bob my head, walking toward my trusty orange van. My eyes turn to saucers the moment I see it, my jaw hanging open in disbelief. Rowan stands there humbly, his hands in his pockets, smiling gently at me in the glowing light.

"Go look around." He tilts his head toward the van, breaking me from my trance.

The doors sit wide open, leaving the inside on full display. I pace closer to inspect what I see. Immaculate strings of twinkle lights line the van's ceiling, illuminating the once-dark interior. My eyes take in every inch, gasping in awe when I notice the floor is no longer rusty but covered in thin, wooden planks. An elevated bed sits on crates, all neatly packed with the items I left in the van. There's even a dog bed on the floor. My eyes mist over as I wring my hands together, too nervous to touch anything. I come up empty for words and slowly turn to face Rowan.

You were wrong, Scar. He is not like them. Not one

bit.

"Do you like it?" Rowan asks, his smile turning into a nervous, straight line as he starts showing me features. "The bed is big enough for two, but I figured Daisy would want her own bed too."

My eyes follow him as he moves gracefully to the other side of the van.

"And if you lift this cushion up, there's compartments inside. It's cedar lined, so it'll keep your clothes safe. And the string lights, they run off a few batteries right here. I've included extras in case these die on you." He pauses, the battery pack in his grip.

I freeze, biting my cheeks hard to ensure that this isn't a dream. "I don't understand . . ."

Rowan sweetly holds out the battery pack toward me, sliding it open. "You have to put the double As in here—"

I cut him off with a small laugh and place my hand lightly on his arm. "No, I don't understand *this*. You did all of this . . . for *me*?" My fingers nervously play with the fabric of my skirt as I look at him.

He takes a moment, then sets the battery pack back where it was neatly stashed. He looks at the van, then back at me, as if it's no big deal, like he merely bought me a travel mug for my trip. Does he even realize he's created a *home* for me?

"You and Daisy deserve somewhere nice to sleep. And when it rains, you can sit inside and read or whatever you like to do." His voice is low as his hands find his pockets. "I couldn't bear the thought of you driving this thing all the way across the country the way it was. I mean, I don't know what you were thinking."

"Why, though? I mean . . . we aren't . . ." I don't want to finish the sentence.

Rowan lets out a little sigh, reaching up to my face, pushing a stray lock of hair behind my ears. His fingers linger at my ear for a moment, causing my heart to race. "I don't need a label to do something nice for someone I care about."

I take a moment to survey every detail. The craftsmanship alone is something to be applauded, but the reality that Rowan built this for me floods me with more emotions and thoughts than I know what to do with.

"So this is why you've been avoiding me for the last few days?" I tease, my hands cocked on my hips.

"I know it was a jerk move to ghost you like that, but once I found out you were one-hundred-percent leaving on Friday, I had to work around the clock. I knew if we talked too long, I'd blow the surprise."

"Did everyone know about this? Gramps . . . Lola . . . Lu?"

"Yeah." He smirks at me. "You mad? I know it's your van, and I probably should've asked for permission, but—"

"I'm not mad," I reply softly. "I'm in shock. This kind of stuff doesn't happen to me. It's like you saw inside my head and created something I've only dreamed of. I don't know how I'll ever pay you back for this." I bite my lip, contemplating my next words. "But at the same time, yeah, I *am* mad. Because I can't get those three days back. And I missed you." I sheepishly gaze up at him.

"Come again?" Rowan leans his head toward me, cupping his ear sarcastically.

"You heard me," I spit back, a mischievous grin blooming on my face.

"You have some time? Right now?"

I nod vigorously. I don't care if it looks desperate. The

guy just built me a home, and I'd be lying if I said I didn't want to spend time with him in it. Even if it breaks my heart in the end.

"Let's take her for a test, then." He winks and slides the van door closed, and I bounce on my toes, barely able to contain my happiness.

I hop into the driver's seat, running my hand over the sparkling dashboard. I'm in total disbelief that my old Volkswagen looks like this. And as we pull out of the parking lot, I can't believe it sounds like this, or rather—what it doesn't sound like. We drive toward the beach, my eyes focused on the cotton-candy sky ahead.

Twenty minutes later, we're pulling off the road onto the packed sand. There are a few other 4x4 vehicles dotted across this stretch of beach, but right here, it's just us. I park sideways so we can soak in the ocean view while sitting inside my beautiful little home. This is a moment I thought would only live in my dreams.

I inch myself up next to Rowan, and we lounge our backs against the bench. My eyes close, and I commit every detail of this moment to memory. Rowan's thumbs strum the back of my hand. My head is against his shoulder, and our feet dangle over the edge together. I want to be nowhere but here, and yet tomorrow I will be hundreds of miles from this spot.

"Wine?" he asks, and I lean up with him as he reaches for a bottle of rosé. The same one in his arms at the grocery store. I smirk, slightly ashamed of how horribly I thought of him at the Piggly Wiggly today. In my defense, I never saw this coming. Any of it.

"So I kind of feel like an ass," I say as he pops it open, pouring it into cups.

"Why's that?" He smiles softly at me.

"I haven't been the best neighbor since I arrived two weeks ago. It took me a moment to realize you weren't . . ." I narrow my eyes to search for the right thing to say, and he sips the wine, puckering his lips. He leans into me, his voice low.

"The enemy?" he adds.

I chuckle. Everything coming from his mouth always sounds serious, like a military mission.

"I was going to say like *the rest of them*. But that's cliché." I wait for a witty remark back, but then he says three unexpected words that reach into my heart and twist it.

"I'll miss you."

My face spins toward him, holding his gaze. I feel like a teenager, falling in love for the first time. Like it's the end of summer and I have to move home. Like the ending roll of credits in a movie that just shattered you.

"I'll miss you too, Rowan. What are you going to do for the rest of the summer?" I ask gently. Part of me knows I'm just asking if he'll remember me.

"Truthfully, I'm not sure." He kicks at the sand. "But I'll be thinking about you. I know that."

The pit in my stomach makes me unsure how to respond, but Rowan leans in to plant another kiss that's so gentle it feels like a feather across my lips. A vibration of tingles rolls up my spine, my breath unsteady as I press my forehead to his. Rowan's thumb swipes across my cheek as a tear rolls down my face, a single tear that holds all the emotion I've been carrying today.

He doesn't back away before whispering something else. "Will you get Thai takeout with me? Every single day for a week?"

"What? Why'd you say that?" I move back slightly, wondering if I heard him right.

"Because you're wrong." Rowan nods as he talks against my lips.

"I'm wrong? About what?" I tease, my eyebrows shooting up.

"You said I'd leave you. But that's not true. I'd never leave you, Scarlett Ray."

"Don't make promises you can't keep, Rowan," I whisper back, a familiar sadness creeping up. Rowan leans back so we can see each other clearly before clearing his throat.

"I *can* promise you one thing, Scar. I'm going to take you on a date, or seven in a row. It doesn't matter if you're back in six weeks or six months. Thai food, just you and me." He is looking right at me, but I stare out past him at the endless ocean.

"What if I don't come back?" I say, my throat tightening the minute those words escape my lips.

"Then I'll fly to you. You think they have good Thai in California?" he jokes, but I know he's serious, causing more tears to spill over.

Rowan holds my head in his hands. I nod against them.

"It's a date," I promise him.

Chapter Eighteen

At quarter to eight, I slide the van door shut, turning to look up at the house once more. The morning sun creeps over the black roof of the house. *I'll be back. I promise.*

"You have everything, kiddo?" Gramps asks, shuffling down the front steps toward me. I nod. I've been up since five this morning, incessantly checking I have everything. I could barely sleep after coming home from the beach with Rowan.

"Call me as soon as you get to camp tonight, okay? And anytime. Call me." He pulls me into a hug, and I cling to him, burying my face in his shoulder. I breathe in, committing his smell to memory and blink hard.

"Thanks for everything, Gramps. I've loved having this time with you. Promise to call *me*, and don't miss a doctor's appointment, okay?" I pray I don't start crying again. He nods, and I have to look away from his glassy eyes.

"Love you," he says, his voice clipped.

"Love you," I reply, my head swinging to the side at the sound of Lola's front door creaking open. We both turn to watch her scamper down the steps and across the lawn with a big brown bag in her arms.

"I was so afraid I would miss your send-off!" She hollers, and I can't hide my grin. I *might* actually miss Lola. The front door swings open again and Rowan comes walking out, greeting me with a layered smile. He has on running shoes and blue shorts. I think about the first time I saw him running on the road. Now that, I'll miss.

"Lola, you didn't have to do this," I coo as she hands me the brown bag, listing off the contents on her fingers.

"Coffee cake, the cinnamon rolls your Gramps said you love, a fruit salad . . . Hmm, what else?" She runs a hand through her blonde bedhead. "Turkey club and a few bones for Miss Daisy!" She smiles, and I look over at Daisy, who is wiggling around Rowan's legs excitedly. He squats down to rub her soft belly.

"Thank you. I can't tell you how much I appreciate it, Lola." And I do. Lola will never be my Mimi, but it doesn't take away from the fact she makes Gramps happy or that she cares about me.

I set the bag in the middle of the front seats, knowing damn well I'll be digging into those cinnamon rolls the moment I drive off.

Gramps and Lola eye each other, then walk toward Gramps's porch.

"We'll let you two say goodbye." Lola winks at me, then throws a look to Rowan. I blush and wave goodbye again.

They walk into the house together, and Rowan stands up, walking toward me with Daisy following him.

I lean back against the van door, looking up at him. His jaw stiffens, but his hazel eyes are intense as they peer into mine. My mouth twitches into a quick smirk because I have nothing to say to him he doesn't already know.

He tips his head down and kisses me torturously slow. He knows what he's doing. I peel my back off the van, and his arms instinctively wrap around me, holding me close.

"Scarlett?"

"Hmm?" I hum back, loving the way my name sounds on his lips.

"Go see your sunset," Rowan whispers in my ear, and my eyes trace up his neck until our gaze meets.

I watch him wave goodbye at the end of the driveway as I drive away. Daisy's head hangs out the window, looking back at him, and a tightness takes over my throat the moment he disappears from sight.

The van feels quiet, and I grip the wheel with both hands, focusing my eyes on the road ahead.

Chapter Nineteen

T hree hours and twenty minutes; that's how long I'm in the van before I pull off into a highway rest stop. I could've kept driving now that I have air conditioning keeping me cool and no rattling noises to plague my anxious mind. But I am one exit away from crossing into South Carolina, and my hands jerked the wheel in reaction when I realized that. Leaving the state feels too final. I need a quick break.

"Wanna stretch, girl?" I turn around to ask Daisy. She has taken up permanent residence on the fluffy, pink dog bed Rowan put on the floor in the van. I didn't have the heart to tell him how impractical that would be for a messy dog like Daisy.

"Come on. Let's go!" I roll open the side door, and Daisy straightens her legs out, arching her back like a cat. I lean down to get the leash out of her designated bin, but my hand lands on the empty bottle of wine I forgot Rowan stashed last night.

"Oh, um . . . ," I stutter, an unexpected flutter in my stomach. Quickly, I toss the pink bottle in the recycling bin a few feet behind the van. I stare at the bin, and for a split second, I want to fish it back out, just so I have something to remind myself it was real, but I don't.

The grass is soft underfoot as I stretch with Daisy, bargaining with my mind to pause its incessant unease for just a moment. She rolls on her back, and I pull my vibrating phone from my pocket.

Rowan: You forgot these.

A text from Rowan lights up my screen. He's sent a picture of my gas-station pink sunglasses sitting in his hands. I let out a little laugh and palm my forehead. I must've left them on Lola's porch last night when we were saying goodnight. There wasn't much talking as much as there was kissing happening, so it's no wonder I forgot them. They cost me ten bucks. I can replace them. Though, they are my favorite pair. My lucky sunglasses. I *probably* shouldn't drive across the country without something lucky.

I round up Daisy, and we get back in the van. The maps app is glaring brightly at me, and my eyes dart from it to the time on the analog clock on my dash and then to Daisy, slobbering on the side door. I make her sit up front with me. It's a long drive, and I need someone to talk to.

The robotic voice from the maps app keeps telling me to turn right to leave the rest stop and get back on the highway. But my hands don't move from my lap, and my eyes stare straight ahead. Five minutes goes by like that.

A whiney noise comes from my throat, and I snatch my phone from the holder, scrolling until I find the number for the camp I'm supposed to check into in three hours. I tap on their phone line, impatiently waiting as it rings and rings and rings. Finally someone answers.

"Hi, my name is Scarlett Peterson. I reserved a spot tonight, but I wanted to let you know I'll be late."

The man on the other end assures me that's not an issue and that I can pay for my spot in the morning. I thank him and hang up, then type a quick text to Rowan.

Scarlett: I knew I forgot something! Thanks, Rowan :)

I catch a glimpse of Daisy, looking at me, expectantly.

"What?" I ask, averting my eyes back to my phone, hastily trying to find my playlist, my fingers shaky.

"It's only a few hours. You'll be fine," I say, hitting play and peeling out of the rest stop. I turn left.

I have to grip the steering wheel tightly to keep my hands from shaking as the van rolls over the bridge connecting the mainland to the island. The afternoon sun glistens off the rippling water underneath, and I take deep breaths in, but it's useless against my growing nerves.

Muscle memory guides me back to the street I left only this morning. I don't look at myself in the rearview mirror. If I do, I'll psych myself out.

I've had three hours to decide this is a good idea. And three hours before that to convince myself it wasn't. Now I've decided *this* is the craziest thing I've ever done. Not driving to California, but *this*.

I leave my van running, the AC blasting inside for Daisy, and run up Lola's front porch steps. Lola's convertible is gone, but Rowan's truck sits unmoved from the driveway.

I beat three rapid knocks on the front door. I bounce on my heels when no one answers immediately and pace across the porch, hands on my hips. Shading my eyes, I lean in to peer through the windows. *Shit, it's completely dark in there.* I should've just called like a normal person.

"No one's gonna answer that door, I'm afraid."

I jump at the sound of that voice and spin around to see Rowan standing at the bottom of the porch steps, breathing hard. Harder than I've ever seen him breathe. His hands are on his hips with nothing but those damn blue jogging shorts on. He looks at me like he's drinking me in. I don't fight the smile spreading across my face.

"You know, I could've mailed you your sunglasses." He smiles between every breath.

"Oh yeah? Well, what about the other thing I forgot? I'm not sure it's shippable," I reply, feeling my pulse rise with every word I say. Nothing is coming out like I rehearsed. Once my eyes landed on Rowan James, it was game over. For both my mind and heart.

"And what would that be?" Rowan's voice is slow and husky as he walks up the porch stairs toward me, stopping only a few feet away.

"You." I said it. All cards on the table.

Neither Rowan nor I move or glance away from each other.

Rowan steps forward, his unwavering eyes erasing every ounce of self-doubt written on my heart. His hands reach around, resting on the back of my neck before he pulls me into him. Our lips crash into each other, and my fingers brush through his damp hair, madly kissing him. Rowan pries away, but not before I get one more nibble of his lip.

166

"You're telling me you came back for *me*?" Rowan asks.

"I've spent too long running from the people who love me. I don't want to make that mistake again."

Rowan says nothing, his hazel eyes stay steady on me while he holds me against him, anchored.

"Say something, Rowan!" I blurt out, ready to shake him.

He cracks a smoldering grin, melting my growing nerves. "I'm speechless, Scar. I didn't think you'd really come back."

"Is that a yes? Will you come with me? Because Daisy is waiting." I smile and nod toward the van, where sure enough, Daisy was watching from the window.

"I mean . . . yes, of course."

Rowan is bewildered but excited. I've successfully ruffled Rowan.

He glances down at his watch. "Give me an hour to pack . . . and shower."

Rowan squeezes me sweetly and lets go. He disappears quickly into the house, and I jog down to the driveway to let Daisy out of the van. She acts like she never left. She follows me to the porch swing on Lola's deck, and we glide back and forth for a little while. Rowan texts me, letting me know he's out of the shower and starting to pack, and I'm about to go see if he needs help when Lola's convertible whips into the driveway. The top is down, and Gramps is riding shotgun. I smile even harder at the image of them. A tiny thought feathers across from my mind. *Maybe that kind of love isn't out of the question for me.*

"Scarlett, what are you doing here? My God, is everything okay?" Gramps asks, slamming the convertible door shut and padding up the steps toward me.

I can't help but laugh, which only causes Gramps's face to grow more confused. He glances at Lola, who just shrugs and follows him up the stairs.

"Everything is fine! Really, it is." I shoot a bashful smile at both of them. "I came back for—"

The front door swinging open interrupts me, and out steps Rowan, his golden-tan skin dewy from the shower. A sight to see.

"I heard the car and thought maybe I should come help explain," Rowan says as he glances toward me, flashing a smoldering grin.

"What am I missing here?" Gramps throws his hands in the air, and I place my hand on his arm.

"I turned around at the South Carolina line, Gramps, because I forgot my sunglasses here."

Gramps looks perplexed, his hands on his hips.

"And I forgot Rowan," I quickly add, turning to look at Rowan.

Lola nearly jumps up and down, grasping at my hand, pulling me into a smothering hug. "I knew it! I knew! Didn't I tell you, Ray?"

"Okay, yes, you called it!" Gramps replies, rolling his eyes but smiling at me.

"Wait a minute, I've been gone for six hours, and y'all are taking bets on me now?" I say, and Lola releases me from the hug but holds me out at an arm's length. Her eyes grow misty as she glances between her nephew and me.

"Oh, come on! The way you two look at each other, I had a feeling you wouldn't go far before you realized it." Lola squeezes my shoulders before grabbing Rowan too. She smooshes us into a group hug that makes Daisy bounce with excitement around us.

"Realize what exactly?" I retort loudly.

"That you're falling in love. You two don't hide it very well." Lola loops her arm through Gramps's.

I chuckle and shake my head. No one said Rowan and I were in love. But neither of us deny it either. Rowan's face is red when I make eye contact with him. It's like we are standing here with our parents, them embarrassing us while we take photos for a high school dance. It's gushy, and I hate how much I kind of love it.

I didn't need to leave to realize I was falling in love with Rowan James. I knew that before today. But it wasn't until I sat at the exit, staring straight ahead, that I truly realized *what* I left behind.

Lola and Gramps insist we don't leave until we are fed a proper lunch, which neither Rowan or I can argue. So we sat down for one more lunch together. Before Lola and Gramps join us at the table, I lean over to Rowan whispering, "Are you sure it's okay to leave them here alone? I feel so selfish stealing you away."

Gramps pinches me on my shoulder as him and Lola round the table, looking at us with their eyebrows raised.

"I may be old, but I can hear you. We will be fine." Gramps winks at me, sitting down as Lola hands him a napkin.

"Rowan is a grown man. I can't keep him here forever," she chimes in and smiles sweetly at him.

"We don't know when we will be back," I start, unable to hide the worry in my voice. I shoot a panicked look at Rowan. Surely, he will want to back out. But he just runs his fingers down my back and shakes his head.

"Be back for Christmas. That's all I care about. You got it?" Gramps says as Lola nods at us and hands me a platter of sandwiches.

I glance at Gramps. He looks at me pensively. He can read me like an open book.

"Everything is going to be okay, Scar." He reaches out and settles a warm hand on mine, a gesture that makes me take a deep breath.

"Thanks, Gramps." I smile and grab a sandwich.

It's really happening.

I should've known Rowan would be organized and methodical. He packed only what he needed and nothing more, fitting everything neatly in his rucksack. We tuck it under the bed in an open spot, like it was always meant to be there.

After another round of hugs and goodbyes, we finally drove away from the island. I let Rowan navigate as I fill him in on all the snacks I have, the playlists I created, and my plans. He graciously listens, never once suggesting anything different.

As we drive along, enjoying each other's company, it's hard for me to wrap my head around how so much has changed in just a few weeks. Or how it's possible I feel so complete right here next to Rowan. Maybe Mimi was right. There is something magical about the ocean. Or perhaps it's always been here and I just had to open my eyes long enough to see it.

Epilogue

R owan gently squeezes my leg, and my eyes flutter
open from his touch. I rub my eyes, waking myself
from what was only supposed to be a twenty-minute nap,
but glancing at the clock, it's been nearly four hours.
My palms rest on top of Rowans, and we exchange soft
smiles.

"You should've woken me up. I didn't want you to have
to drive the entire way alone. I would've switched with
you," I remind him. He gently shrugs him shoulders.

One thing I've learned about Rowan in the last few
weeks is he is determined. Give him a goal, and he com-
pletes it. Even if it means driving through Southern California rush hour to get to the beach so your girlfriend can
see the sunset. Oh, he started calling me his girlfriend
three weeks ago somewhere in Colorado.

"I see it! I see the ocean!" I cry out a few moments later,
banging my hand on the dashboard and nearly bouncing
out of my seat. Daisy springs off the floor between Rowan

and me, stretching her neck to see what the commotion is about.

The deep blue water emerges into view as we coast down Highway One a few miles longer, eventually snagging a coveted parking spot along the public beach access. Flinging my door open, I hop out, balancing on one foot, while hastily pulling my sandals on. Daisy jumps on the seat, tail thumping against the dashboard. I encase her sweet, slobbery face in my hands and plant a kiss between her eyes.

"We made it, Daisy. Just like I promised," I whisper, looping her leash around her neck.

Rowan comes around the van and holds out my beat-up pink sunglasses. "Don't forget these, Scar." He winks, joking with me as I pluck them from his open palm and replace the empty space with my hand.

The three of us walk together toward the wooden steps leading to the rocky shore. We kick off our shoes, and I swivel toward Rowan. I don't have to say anything; he releases my hand, looks longingly at me, and then leans back to sit on the rock. Daisy eyes me impatiently; it's been a while since she's seen the ocean.

And then we ran straight into the Pacific Ocean.

I let out a squeal as the cool water rushes up over my feet, crashing against my legs, and Daisy pounces, determined to bite every wave coming her way. I twirl around, catching Rowan's loving stare, and I scream out his name, beckoning him to join us. He pushes himself off the rock and jogs into the water, capturing my waist and pulling me to him.

"How's it feel to finally see your sunset?" Rowan's voice envelopes me like a warm blanket. He holds me from behind, and I let my head go heavy against his shoulder.

I don't answer Rowan immediately because I don't know if the words exist yet for what's stirring inside of me. So instead, I fill my lungs with salty air and gaze at the horizon through my rose-colored lenses.

This exact moment has played time and time again in my head over the last seven years. Every time I thought I was getting closer to making this dream come true, I'd allow myself to visualize how it would feel to stand here. And even though I'd planned this exact moment with different people, I always envisioned running into the ocean alone. As if it was something special, just for me. Maybe I expected it to change me, to be the pinnacle of my existence thus far.

Even as Rowan and I drove away from the island, Lola and Gramps waving like two proud parents in the driveway, I still pictured it like that. I imagined it like that as Rowan and I grew closer along the road. I pictured having this moment alone until I got here.

Standing here, my feet firmly planted on the sand, I let go of what I pictured for my life and release the grudges I've been holding against myself. Instead, I pull Rowan's arms tighter around me and smile at my sweet Daisy.

Now I see this moment isn't what would make my life better. Instead, every little detour along the way is what shaped my story. As Gramps says, the messy parts in the middle are what define you, and how you react to them. Maybe it was always meant to be this way all along.

Rowan pulls away, and I spin to face him. The sun sits low in the sky, casting shadows on us.

"You owe me a date. I think seven in a row if I remember correctly." I jab my finger into his chest, and he licks his lips, readjusting his baseball cap.

"Is that so?" he asks, and I respond with a kiss.

173

Rowan pulls his phone from his pocket. The screen lights up, showing a Thai restaurant already mapped out. *I should've known he'd already have it planned.* That night, we checked into our rental cottage and ordered Thai. Under the starry sky, we had the date Rowan promised me months ago.

It took us almost eight weeks to get to the West Coast. Eight weeks in a tiny van together, learning each other's quirks. For instance, Rowan uses a paper map and compass when we hike. He also runs at 7:00 a.m., no matter what time we go to bed. He takes his coffee black, and his favorite donut has icing *and* sprinkles. To which I've told him I'd look past since he looks past the fact I've lost the van keys twice.

We haven't been lonely, considering how often Gramps and Lola insist on video-chatting us. It *almost* makes Rowan and I regret teaching them how. They crowd together on the screen, and it's always upside down, or we're only talking to Gramps's shoe half the call. Without fail, Lola tells Rowan he needs to eat more and spills every ounce of town gossip she can in thirty minutes. Gramps simply asks if the van is running smoothly, and surprisingly, I tell him it is.

Our van also gets compliments everywhere we go. People always want to hire Rowan when they find out he outfitted it himself, and I've fallen in love with watching his face light up with humble pride. And though we are taking everything day by day, when we allow ourselves to dream, Rowan talks about maybe pursuing carpentry. I dream about what I'd have in a custom house if *someone* built it for me. He smirks and nods along with all my outlandish ideas, never saying it's impossible. *Maybe someday.*

Five Months Later

I reach out and crank the heat higher. Hot air starts to blow, and I smile, cozying up into my oversized, ugly sweater while gingerly gripping my coffee with both hands.

"You know, if you got hot instead of iced coffee like a normal person, you wouldn't be shivering right now."

I smile but roll my eyes at the unneeded reminder, turning to look down at Daisy seated between us.

"There's no fun in being normal. You should know that by now, Rowan!" I reply dramatically, taking another sip of the ice-cold latte and scratching Daisy's floppy ears.

Rowan laughs but doesn't try to rationalize with me anymore. After seven months together, he's seen it all from me. And he hasn't left. To be fair, he *hasn't* seen me go absolutely mad over Christmas yet, but I did insist on getting matching ugly sweaters for Christmas Eve dinner, and he didn't object. So my chances are still looking good.

"This is how you know I really love you, Scar." He jingles the bells on the obnoxious sweater I persuaded him to wear.

I slap my hand over my mouth, laughing hysterically. Rowan's face turns slightly red, but he lets out a chuckle.

"But really, if you're going to roast us in here, I'm at least going to take this off until we get there."

"Fine by me." I coo, "And I love you too."

Rowan glances at me, a one-sided smirk slowly creeping across his face. He pulls the sweater over his head, exposing his body in the tight, white shirt underneath. I don't hide my ogling eyes, which makes him grin wider.

"Eyes on the road, soldier. The exit is coming up soon!" I tease back.

Another Christmas jingle starts on the radio, so I crank the volume, singing along to every word. Raleigh disappears in the rearview mirror as we merge onto the highway. In a few short hours, we'll pull up to Lola's with a van full of wrapped presents, and tonight we will have Christmas dinner together—Lola, Gramps, Rowan, and I. And Daisy, of course. She's already wearing the new pink sweater Lola sent.

Rowan reaches over Daisy to run his thumb across my cheek. It's a gesture he often does, one I never tire of. It's been two months since beginning in a new city again. But this time is different. I wasn't running from anything or hiding. Not even from myself.

Soon ocean air will fill my lungs, and I'll hug Gramps for the first time since June. I can hardly wait to see his cheerful face. And tell him he was right.

You just know when you know. Home doesn't have to have a geographical location. Home is wherever you close your eyes at night. Home is four paws and a guy who runs

in blue shorts. Home is where you accept every messy bit
of yourself, exactly where you are.

Acknowledgments

First, thank *you*, the reader, for picking this book up and giving it a chance. I am humbled by the love and support I've received thus far in my author career; it's truly heartwarming! This book was born out of a quick trip to the beach with my husband and the desire to write about my home state, North Carolina. Second, I want to thank everyone in the Bookstagram community - all the readers, reviewers, and incredible indie authors who have cheered me on and given advice every step of the way. Thank you to my beta readers, Lindsey and Kat, who never say no when I need a second pair of eyes. To my amazingly supportive editor, Kimberly, thanks for making my writing readable! Also, The Way You See Me wouldn't even exist as the story you know without my beta reader Alli. Thank you for reading, re-reading my story, and giving me honest and kind feedback. I'm so lucky to have found you! And to my husband, who is always the first to read my books. Your love and support are my backbones, and you never fail to remind me how proud you are to call me your wife.

Last but not least, I'm grateful to my sweet dog Wilbur, who lays under my feet while I write and brings me all his toys while I attempt to concentrate. Every girl needs a dog by her side, and without him, I wouldn't have the inspiration for Daisy.

PS: If you enjoyed this book, can I ask you for one more favor? Please share it with a friend or write a review wherever you write reviews! It's a small gesture that genuinely makes a difference for a new author like myself! Always much appreciated!

About Author

Katherine Bitner is the author of *Time To Bloom* and *The Way You See Me.* She comes from a long line of passionate storytellers and loves to write about love – in all forms. When she isn't writing novels or poetry, you can find her traveling with her husband and dog and drinking copious amounts of coffee. She resides in her adopted home state of North Carolina.

You can connect with Katherine on Instagram at *thekatherinebitner* and at *www.katherinebitner.com*

Printed in Great Britain
by Amazon

32167486R00108